About the Author

Carrie Bright is a self-confessed bookaholic and magazine addict. She was born in Wales but later moved to England and settled in South Yorkshire. She felt a bit strange as the 'new girl in school' and would escape between the covers of a book whenever possible. Characters created by E. Nesbit, N. Streatfield and E. Goudge were her friends.

As a teenager she would go round to her (real) best friend's and read all her magazines one after another. They tried out every top tip and fashion feature possible – Carrie seems to remember mixing up a mud coloured lipstick, wearing fashion-victim clothes and wishing she had some of the worries she read about in the problem pages! Going to a girls' school meant she could only dream of romance – which probably inspired some of the *Maddy* stories.

Carrie works part time as a children's librarian. You can visit her website at www.carriebright.co.uk to find our more about *Maddy*, and also about *Jamie B*, a series of books Carrie wrote under her other name, Ceri Worman.

To Kay, Debbie and Jan – forever friends!

With thanks to the pupils of Westborough High School, Dewsbury, who read the manuscript:
Kirran Akhtar, Shannon Barrowcliffe, Emily Benham, Zeba Hussain, Faaiza Khan, Helen Neagle, Asma Patel, Zara Rauf, Neelam Riaz, Henna Sabir, Kiran Sadiq, Sanha Saleem and staff Fiona Bruce and June Rowling as well as Bryony Nixon of Kingstone School, Barnsley.

ORCHARD BOOKS
338 Euston Road, London NW1 3BH
Orchard Books Australia
Level 17, 207 Kent Street, Sydney, NSW 2000, Australia

ISBN: 978 1 84616 327 2

First published in 2007 by Orchard Books
A paperback original

A CIP catalogue record for this book is available from the British Library.

1 3 5 7 9 10 8 6 4 2
Printed in Great Britain

The paper and board used in this paperback are natural recyclable products made from wood grown in sustainable forests. The manufacturing processes conform to the environmental regulations of the country of orgin.

Orchard Books is a division of Hachette Children's Books
www.orchardbooks.co.uk

Jealousy Junkie

cringes, confessions and caught-on-camera clangers!

Carrie Bright

ORCHARD BOOKS

Hi, it's Maddy Blue here and I'm a total mag-hag - addicted to magazines!

When I'm feeling mad, sad or bad I buy myself one, crawl between the bright, shiny pages and get lost forever. (Mad's note: Some people wish I would...)

If my life was a magazine would it be a glitzy, glossy number full of fabulous fashion-shoots? Or a down-market cheapie, complete with cringes and caught-on-camera clangers?

You be the judge. Here's my life in a magazine. (Well, kind of.) I cut up some mags and used them up to customise the story. Then I added some doodly decor and Mad notes.

Hope you enjoy it!

Maddy x

The World's Top Teen Magazine!

written, edited, designed and published by

Maddy Blue

Issue No. 1:

Jealousy Junkie!

A MADDY BLUE PRODUCTION

[illegible]

[illegible]

[illegible]

[illegible]

1

FRIENDSHIP FORECAST

by *Destiny Dreamer*

Leo

Two's company but is three a crowd?
There's a shooting star zooming into your planetary area. It means a new person will enter your life, but can an old friendship stand the test?

Wear something sparkly for luck.

Spoooooky!
Last night I painted my toe nails with sparkly nail polish for the first time ever! It's a sign – a sparkly sign!

OK so it was a free gift with this mag but so what? According to my stars someone new is going to zap into my life.

'Maddy – Scott's here!' Mum shouts up.

I close my mag, cram it in my school bag and go downstairs in my usual daze.

Who can this new person possibly be? And what did Destiny Dreamer mean, *'can an old friendship stand the test?'*

You can't get a much older friend than Scott. Not that he's ancient – he's the same age as me – what I mean is that we've been friends forever.

No one could possibly come between us.

'Science test today. Got your book?' Scott says as I get to the door.

I turn around, go back upstairs and rescue it from under a pile of magazines.

'And don't forget your umbrella – it looks like rain!' he adds as I come back down.

'Rain? *Nooo*, can my life get any worse!'

'Come on drama diva – it's just drizzle.'

'Yeah, but drizzle means frizzle and I've just done my hair! You know what happens when it gets wet – *hair-scare nightmare.*'

'Well, go get your brolly or we'll be late for school!'

'S'OK. It's in my bag. Last week's free gift from one of my magazines.'

'Well at least they've got some use,' Scott mutters as he shuts the front door and we set off to Westfield High.

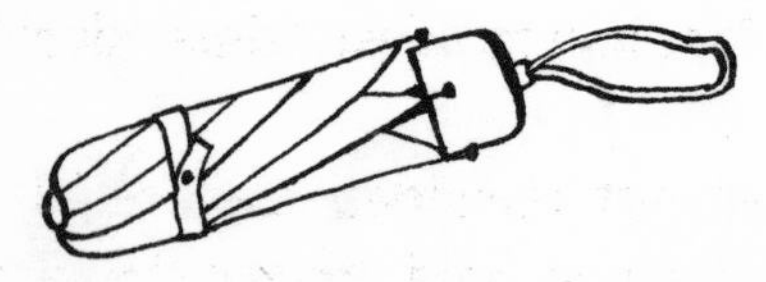

'So, did you revise last night?' Scott asks as we walk our usual route.

'Mmm well, I tried to but then I sort of got distracted by my new mag. I had to check out my stars...'

'Yeah, but that only takes two minutes! So what stopped you revising?'

'Oh, you know, then I glanced at one or two more pages...the *Top Ten Tips for a Dream-Date Diva* and the *True Confessions of a Psycho-Teen Killer* and the *Dish-The-Dirt Diary* of this girl who married her best friend's dog—'

'Maddy, why do you read that trash? What's the point?'

'It's not trash, Scott. It's REAL LIFE! I feel sorry for boys... How do you know what to try and what to buy, who's in and who's out, what's hot and what's not if you don't read mags?'

'And how do you know the Periodic Table, Newton's Third Law and the life cycle of a fruit fly if you don't study?'

'Oh, get real Scott. What's the use of knowing all that stuff? Um...you will sit next to me in the science test, won't you? And make sure you write in extra big letters, too.'

'Yes and I'll be your private surgeon when you need that brain implant in a few years' time. After all, what are friends for?'

'Ooh, you've just reminded me. Friends... Listen to this, Destiny Dreamer said there'd be a new person coming into my life. It's all to do with a star shooting into my planetary area...'

'Sounds painful,' Scott says, dragging me past a newsagent's before I can sneak a peek at the mags.

'Aww, come on Scott, just five minutes. Maybe this new person's in that shop right now and—'

'Or maybe the new person is the teacher on late duty today. You can get to know them better at lunchtime detention...but if that's not in your *Cosmic Plan*, keep walking and stop talking. Oh, and get your brolly out. It's frizz-alert time.'

'Aaaagh!' I manage to keep walking, screaming and scrabbling about in my bag at the same time. Finally I have to give up.

'Scott, stop!' I say, taking shelter from the rain in a doorway. 'Someone's stolen my umbrella – I'm sure I put it in my bag last night...or did I?'

He pauses briefly, whips out an umbrella and opens it. 'Let's go!'

But I can't move. My mouth has twisted into an extra-wide cover-girl smile.

'Scott? I don't *believe* it! Who would have guessed you were a brolly-dolly! And purple polka dots are *so* your style.'

'Don't push it, baby. Mum made me take it this morning. And no one argues with Nurse Hyacinth Lord on the warpath. Not that I need it, a bit of rain never hurt anyone...' He starts to close the umbrella again.

'No, wait!' I dodge under it and we huddle up as he opens it out again. *'Thankyou-thankyou-thankyou,* Scott. Where would I be without you?'

'Wet!'

We don't say much more till we get to school.

Scott's fast and focussed and I'm fat and breathless trotting at his side to keep up.

We reach the school gates just before the bell goes.

'You'd better ditch the purple hair-protector now,' I say, even though it's still raining. 'Don't want to ruin your image...'

This is the ultimate sacrifice – I'm still risking frizz-factor 8 (on a scale of 1–10) with the short walk across the school yard.

'It's cool,' Scott says. 'Let them laugh. We've come this far. Like I said, what are friends for?'

Typical Scott. Still looking out for me – he's done that ever since nursery. We met when he told this big kid to give my Barbie doll back. I stopped crying and made Scott laugh by getting Barbie to chat up his dumper truck.

At that time, my doll was my only friend. Since then it's been me and Scott against the world.

Just like now – clutching the polka-dot parasol and holding our heads high as we walk to the school door. Yes, we get one or two funny looks but anyone else would be laughed off the planet.

Of course it helps that Scott's tall and broad and he's not afraid to speak out (except where his mum's involved!) People take him seriously. They must do – he just got voted our class rep on the school council.

Me, I'm invisible. I'm just the dumpy girl who hangs round with him. Everyone else goes around in groups and gangs and no one notices me at all – which is just how I like it!

We get to class before the teacher, and Scott decides to help me yet again, 'If you get your science book out I can test you before Miss Bruce gets here.'

Sigh... He means well, I know it but...*double sigh...* The day stretches ahead of me as dull and grey as the school uniform I'm forced to wear.

Nothing's changed.

What happened to that new person my mag promised this morning?

If Destiny Dreamer's words don't come true, can I get a refund?

Just then a teacher pokes his head round the door. 'Miss Bruce will be a few minutes late,' he says. 'So please wait quietly and show how well you can behave. She's just going to collect the new pupil from reception.'

'Sir, who is it? Boy or girl?' someone asks.

'Girl. The name's Starr. Starr Child,' the teacher replies.

Spookerama!

Suddenly my brain starts fizzing like a bath bomb. Is this the shooting star zapping into my life...?

(Mad's note: Read Destiny Dreamer* every week - she's so right it's scary!)

(*Terms and conditions apply. Always read the smallprint.)

2

RATE YOUR MATE

What's their score?

20/20

Is your friendship rock solid? Take this quiz together and find out if you'll be friends for life or friends till lunchtime.

'OK what is Newton's Third Law?' Scott says, opening up his science book.

I look at him blankly. 'Starr? *Starr Child?* That can't be her real name, can it? It's too much of a coincidence.'

'Tcha!' Scott sucks his teeth impatiently. 'Wat'cha on about, girl?'

We've been friends for so long that he doesn't even bother to be polite any more. I ignore him and carry on. 'If it is her real name, I bet that (a) her parents are faded pop-stars (b) they're old-school hippies or (c) she's fallen to earth from another planet. You choose.'

I choose Science. Newton's Third Law, remember? I'll give you a clue, *'For every action, there is an equal but opposite...'*

'Who knows?' I shrug my shoulders. 'Strange and spooky things happen out there in the universe.'

'Maddy, you can't put that in the test! Listen, *Newton's Third Law: "For every action, there is an equal but opposite reaction".*'

'Nope don't get it. Oh...you mean like if someone enters your life that's an action. Quite a radical one really.'

'Yee-esss, I suppose, and—?'

'So that's going to cause a reaction...like something radical's going to happen because of it?'

'In theory yes, but we're talking physics and—'

I don't hear the rest. I'm thinking of Destiny Dreamer's words about this new star in my life.

Can an old friendship stand the test?

That's what she said. So, what if this new girl wants to be my friend? How will Scott react? Will he be jealous? Will we fall out? Now I'm getting really spooked.

I look around. Everyone's chatting and there's no sign of Miss Bruce yet.

'Quick, Scott. There's a five-minute friendship test in this week's mag. Let's have a go!'

'Maddy, are you mad? Think about the future. What's more important to you – an educational science test or a trashy magazine test...?'

He looks at me. I look at him and he closes his science book.

'OK, stupid question. Let's get on with it...'

Five minutes later we've both filled in our answers and

I'm adding up the scores. 'Wow, Scott, listen to this...

Top marks 20/20 Friends for Life

Lifecoach Laura says **Congratulations!**

- You have a friendship based on trust, loyalty and a sense of humour.

- You understand each other and enjoy being together so much, you're like twins!'

'That's so true, isn't it – I told you mags aren't rubbish!' I say, but Scott's laughing like a maniac.

'That just proves my point! In case you hadn't noticed, I'm a black teenage boy and and you're a white teenage girl. *Twins?*... I don't think so!'

'You know what it means,' I say, feeling relieved. 'We're true best friends and that's the way it's going to stay.'

Yep, even if this new star does come zapping into my zone causing strange reactions, we're safe. Our friendship will definitely stand the test – the mag says so.

Suddenly the door flies open and Miss Bruce walks in, closely followed by the new girl. The class chat fades to

a hush because we're desperate to check her out.

She's very suntanned (without a streak in sight) and you can't miss her long, bronzed legs because she's wearing flowery flip-flops. Her hair is *sun-kissed blonde* (like the wash-out colour dye) but it looks really natural. It's tumbling out of her pony tail in long, thick waves. She's wearing school uniform like the rest of us but with her figure looks like this month's must-have fashion item.

Yep, I think you've got the picture. This *golden girl* must be Starr Child. She just sort of...glows.

Miss Bruce carries on talking to her while the rest of us listen in stunned silence. '...and the school day starts at nine a.m. on the dot. So if you can get here a little earlier tomorrow?'

Starr opens her big amber eyes wide. 'Oh, sorry, Miss. We only got back from Spain last night. The plane was late and we all overslept this morning.'

She's talking extra-fast and waving her hands around. Her rings flash and her bangles jangle as she carries on, 'We had to wait for a taxi because—'

'OK, fill me in later. Now, what about your school shoes?'

Starr looks down at her flip-flops and gasps. Everyone laughs but she doesn't look embarrassed. I reckon she's enjoying the attention. 'Oh I am *soo* sorry! I can't believe I did that – I got dressed in a total rush this morning. We're staying in a hotel till we can move into *Bar Salsa* and—'

'Yes, I see,' Miss Bruce cuts in just as this is getting interesting. 'Please sort your shoes out for

tomorrow and take those rings and bracelets off before your first lesson.'

Then she waves Starr over to the empty desk in front of me and Scott.

Blusherama!!

If she sits in front of me we'll look like the *Before* and *After* photos in a makeover feature. Just looking at Starr makes me feel frizzier, **fatter** and spottier than ever.

Luckily she sits in front of Scott, so I'm saved the competition. All eyes are on her as she takes off her rings and bangles. She's piling them up on her desk like it's a market stall.

Miss Bruce finishes the register and looks at her watch.

'Only a few minutes before your first lesson, so let's welcome Starr Child to our class. It's not easy starting at a new school so I want someone to show her around for the week and keep an eye on her.'

A whole sea of hands goes up – quite a few boys fancy keeping an eye on Starr, I notice. My hands stay firmly in my lap. Me, show Starr around for a week? It's like everlasting lipstick – great in theory, but it just ain't gonna happen.

Starr's not my type at all. She's pretty and confident and deeply, deeply tanned. Everything I'm not and never will be...

(Mad's note: Redheads only have to look at the sun and they burn to a frizzled freckle.)

It sounds mean but I don't rate her... I hate her.

Anyway, why would Miss Cover-girl Perfect want to

be friends with a misfit like me?

'It's lovely to see so many volunteers,' Miss Bruce says, 'but I think Scott Lord, our school council rep, should look after Starr.'

There's a big cheer and a few whistles. Starr turns round to Scott, flashing her big eyes and smiling like a toothpaste ad.

He looks a bit embarrassed but I don't know why. I saw him put his hand up along with the others. Why didn't he ask me before he landed us with Supermodel Starr?

'We know what it's like to be on the outside, don't we Maddy?' he whispers, but I say nothing.

Remember that five-minute friendship test?

Top marks?

Huh!

Scott just wiped ten whole points off his score...

Friends for life?

Hah!

With Starr as competition we'll be lucky if we make it till lunchtime.

3

D'YOU WANNA BE IN MY GANG?

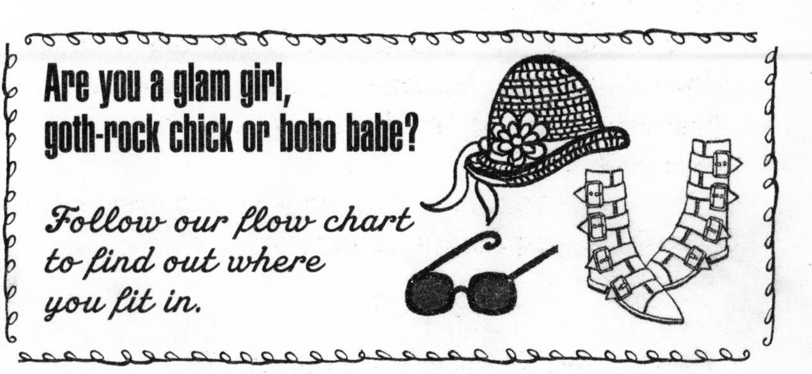

OK, so we make it till lunchtime. Starr sticks with us and Scott is his usual helpful self, showing her where to go and helping her fit in. This is one of the reasons I like him – he's so responsible and caring – but today it makes me feel very twitchy.

Can an old friendship stand the test?

Now we're sitting in the school café making a cosy threesome. Scott's got his usual meat feast, I'm tucking into a healthy option meal with low-fat dressing and super-slim Starr's got a plate piled high with carbs. Life is so unfair!

'So how does Westfield High compare to your other schools?' Scott asks Starr, politely.

'Mmm, pretty much the same,' she says, polishing off the last of her deep-crust pizza and starting on the chocolate cake. 'My parents ran a few pubs in London and then we moved abroad so I've never really been at one school for more than a year.'

Scott nods sympathetically. 'So how long d'you think you'll be here then?'

Starr shrugs her shoulders and bites into another piece of cake. 'Mmm dunno. For ever, I hope. We're making a new start with the salsa bar after what happened in Spain.'

'Why what happened?' I ask. Scott gives me a look but Starr doesn't seem to mind.

'We had this club called *Starspace* and it was doing really well. All the best DJs and queues every night to get in....but Matt's business partner took off with all the money and left us with nothing but a load of bills to pay.'

'And Matt is?' Scott asks.

'Oh, sorry – he's my dad. He's from Westfield, so that's why we're here. His parents are his new business partners. They've put up the money for *Bar Salsa* and it'll take years to pay them back.'

She pushes her plate away. *Snack-attack!* There's still half a mountain of cake left! How can she just abandon it like that? I get this sudden chocoholic craving and fight the urge to open my mouth and hoover it up, plate and all.

Instead I do what I always do in a crisis. *When in*

doubt, get your mag out! It's never failed me yet...

I flick it open and then I see it, the perfect solution. 'Ooh look a friendship flow chart! First question to Starr.

When you go out, do you wear...

a. The latest high street fashion?
b. Black with an added touch of black?
c. Something floaty, possibly with bells?'

'Maddy, I'm not sure Starr wants to do a magazine quiz right now. She's just settling in – give her a chance...'

'But Scott, you know how hard it is to break into all the different groups in school. This will help Starr find out where she fits in best!'

(Mad's note: And drop her off our friendship radar.)

'Sure, sounds like fun!' Starr says. Scott just rolls his eyes while I repeat the question.

'High street, black or floaty? a, b, or c?'

'You know, I prefer to poke around charity shops to find stuff. You can pick up some great vintage pieces. Or sometimes I customise my clothes to make them unique. So, I guess it's none of the above.'

Yeuch! Poke around charity shops? That's just like my

mother! I always wait outside when she does that and pretend I'm not with her.

Second-hand clothes? Starr calls them *vintage*, Mum calls them *bargains.* I call them *smelly.* Same difference.

'OK, er, let's try the next one then.

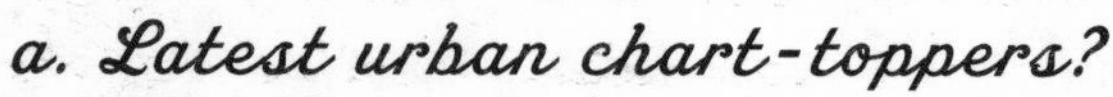

What type of music do you listen to:

a. Latest urban chart-toppers?
b. Headbangin' rock tunes preferably about death?
c. Airy, fairy love songs?'

'Oh, sorry. I'm a bit out of touch at the moment. Matt and Honey ran this bar in Spain for some friends this summer, so I'm into salsa. Is that on the flow chart?

'No, Starr. You're off the chart on that one.'

'So, can you dance South-American style?' Scott's mouth is hanging open and I don't think it's the school dinner that's making him drool.

Starr nods.

Nooo. She's a dancer, too! Why can't she have a nice unsexy hobby like stamp-collecting or train-spotting?

'I believe that salsa has its roots in slavery,' Scott says, as if his interest is purely historical.

Starr looks ready to answer him but we haven't finished

the flow chart yet! Starr's got to fit into one of these friendship groups, hasn't she?

'This one's easy, Starr. You'll definitely get a friendship quick-fit with this.

When you hang out with your mates, what do you like to do:

a. Watch the latest TV soaps?
b. Dye your hair black and sit around being tragic?
c. Go for long walks to look at the clouds?'

Starr doesn't say anything to this. In fact her face looks as blank as the tick boxes on my page. I wait a bit but the silence stretches out like a celebrity smile.

Maybe she didn't hear me? I try again,

'When you hang out with your mates, what do you—'

'Every year the school rep has to raise money for charity so I need to think of some kind of event. Any ideas, both of you?' Scott interrupts me in full flow.

Was it something I said? Ok, I know Scott thinks my mag quizzes are pointless but did he have to cut in like that?

'What happened last time?' Starr asks. Nothing wrong with her hearing, then.

'Er, someone organised a fun run, I think,' Scott says.

'Hah! *Fun* run? What's funny about running through a mud bath in the driving rain?' I shudder at the memory of goosebumps and frizzy hair. 'This year has *got* to be different. We need glamour and glitz. We need romance and razamatazz. We need—'

I'm flicking through my mag now, desperate for an idea. It's full of buy-me-now boots, bags and belts...

'A fashion show!' I sing out, triumphantly.

'And how do we make money out of it?' Scott asks. 'It's for the children's ward at Westfield Hospital, don't forget.'

Scott's mum is a nurse there so that's why he chose it. He's got a point. Money. *Hmm...*

'You could buy cheap clothes in the sales or at charity shops and customise them,' Starr says. 'Then get students to model them and auction them off to the highest bidder,' she adds looking very pleased with herself.

'More dash than cash,' I mutter.

'*More dash than cash!* Great idea, but can we organise it for the end of next month?'

I nod.

Starr nods.

Scott smiles, '*Yes!*' He pulls a pen out of his pocket and scribbles on the back of a napkin saying, 'I'll talk to Miss Bruce today...this is what it's all about – team work!'

When he's finished he gives us both a hug. *Awww!* We're just one big happy family. So why do I feel so down?

I close my mag – it looks like Starr doesn't need the friendship flow chart after all. She doesn't fit into any of the boxes and I think she's found her 'friends' already. But I'll keep it for an emergency.

If three turns out to be too much of a tight squeeze then I'll need to find a new friendship group.

Trouble is, I don't think I fit into an a, b or c box either. I'll probably end up in an m box.

m for 'misfit'

Population = 1

4

TOP THREE TIPS TO BE A MODEL!

TOP MODEL TIPS – NUMBER 1

It's hard work and not everyone's got what it takes. There might be some setbacks along the way...
But if you make it to the top, the rewards are fantastic! Designer clothes, exotic travel and you get to date the world's best-looking guys...
Still interested?

'Are you going to put your name down as a model?' Scott asks a week or two later. 'It's all in a good cause...'

Starr's being picked up by car today so the two of us are walking home together. Me and Scott, just like old times – *awww!*

'Me, a model? Are you having a laugh? I'm fat, frizzy and five foot four. Hardly model material. The only thing I'd look good in is a sack!'

'Oh come on, Maddy. This is Westfield High charity show, not London fashion week! We just want ordinary people.'

'Yeah, thanks very much. That makes me feel a whole lot better.'

'I didn't mean it like that! I mean you're...natural, not all fake and make-up. That's what we're looking for.'

I smile.

'And you've got a great smile!'

'You really think I could have a go? Maddy the model?'

''Course I do. You once told me your dream is to be a catwalk queen. You had your nose in a magazine at the time, I seem to remember. Well, now's your chance.'

TOP MODEL TIPS – NUMBER 2

Are you a catwalk queen?
Can you keep cool with all eyes on you and a thousand cameras flashing?
Do you ooze attitude and confidence?
If so, you're halfway there!

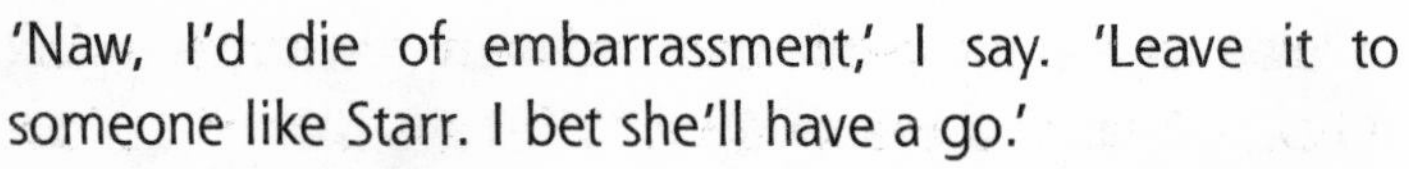

'Naw, I'd die of embarrassment,' I say. 'Leave it to someone like Starr. I bet she'll have a go.'

'Well I'll ask her too, but what about you, Maddy? I know it's what you want. You can't bury yourself in the pages of a magazine forever. You gotta *get real and live the dream!*'

For a second there Scott's got me going. I'd love to float down a catwalk feeling like a star...

Then I catch sight of myself in a shop window. Back to reality – Maddy Blue the model? No, a real-life mag world is not for girls like me.

I shake my head.

'C'mon, last chance or I'll put your name down myself.'

'You wouldn't!'

'Wouldn't I?'

He's probably joking but I decide to play along with him, just in case.

'When do the names have to be in?'

'By Friday after school.'

'Hmm OK... Anyway, what about you, Scott? You could strut your stuff on the stage, too!'

'Not me!' Scott looks shocked and gets all formal. 'I'm certainly not the male-model type.'

'Why not? You've got lots going for you – tall, good-looking, all-year tan—'

Scott wallops me for that.

'Sorry, but it's true – listen to Maddy Blue, your style guru! And you'd look even better if you grew your hair – afro, cornrows, dreadlocks...'

Scott sucks his teeth and puts on his street voice. *'Chah – I ain't no beauty queen!'* The he gets all serious again. 'You're talking to a future lawyer here. Leave me to do the organising and I'll leave the catwalk to you.'

So Friday comes around and I really wish I had the nerve to put my name down as a model but I don't. It doesn't help to have Starr hanging round with us all the time either – does she ever have a bad hair day?

Luckily Scott's too busy to check up on me – he's stressing about the show all the time. 'There's a lot to think about. The three of us need to sit down properly and have a planning meeting at the weekend,' he says one lunchtime.

'Well, we've moved into *Bar Salsa* now, so why don't you both come over to mine?' Starr says.

'Thanks that'd be great, but are you sure your parents won't mind?'

'It's no problem, really. I hardly see Matt and Honey at all they're so busy downstairs in the bar. We've got a private flat on the top floor, so we won't be disturbed.'

'So, Matt and Honey, they're – like – your mum and dad?' I say. 'But you don't call them that?'

'No, they've always been Matt and Honey to me,' Starr laughs. 'I guess it's from when I was little and I saw Honey on TV.'

'On TV?'

'Oh, it was just some reality TV show. After she stopped modelling she tried to revive her career by appearing on it, but it didn't really work.'

'After she stopped modelling...?' I know I sound like Little Miss Echo here, but this is too much to take in.

'Mmm, she did some glamour modelling and promotions work. Then she got this big contract and went out to Spain. That's where she met Matt, when he was busking in Madrid. It was very romantic – a model

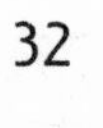

and a musician – till she got pregnant and it all sort of fell apart. She wasn't well for a while after she had me.'

'So your mum was a model? A *real* model?' (It's Little Miss Echo again.)

'Sort of, but it's no big deal. It was years ago, anyway. She gave up on fame after the TV show. So, are you both coming over on Sunday?'

Scott and Starr start making arrangements but I'm on another planet. Starr's mum was a model! Why didn't I guess? You've only got to look at her to see it's true.

And I bet Starr will follow in her fashionable footsteps. After all, she's got what it takes. I should know – I'm not a mag-hag for nothing.

TOP MODEL TIPS – NUMBER 3

Join the Top Modelling Agency Skin and Bones. We are looking for girls who are:

- *Long and leggy (over six foot is ideal)*
- *Size 2 – maximum dress size*
- *Sculpted – with cheek bones like chipped marble*
- *If you've got what it takes then what are you waiting for?*

Contact us now!

(Mad's note: OK, the mag didn't really say this, but you get the idea...)

So, I only hope Scott didn't think again and put my name down as a model after all.

Imagine competing on the same stage as Starr! If your mother's a model you're practically *born* in high heels...

(Mad's note: Ouch!)

5

ARE YOU A JEALOUSY JUNKIE?

When your new mate invites you round to her place do you secretly hope it's a run-down hovel?

Take our envy exam if you dare!

'Do we have to go over to Starr's bar today?' I ask when Scott calls round for me on Sunday. 'Remember that old pub that used to be there before – *The Dirty Rascal*? It had a really dodgy reputation... How do we know that *Bar Salsa*'s any different? Maybe we should ring her and cancel?'

'But this meeting's important, Maddy. We can't cancel now. Are you sure that's what's bothering you?'

I shrug. 'Yeah – why, what d'you mean?'

'I mean you don't mind Starr going round with us, do you? She seems keen to help out. Is that a problem?'

'No, 'course not.'

And when he puts it like that I feel really selfish. Starr is trying to fit in with us and help out. She does seem to be a really nice person, so what's wrong with me?

'S'pose I'm used to it being just the two of us, that's all,' I admit.

'Yeah, but that doesn't mean we can't have other friends, too, does it? We're still best mates aren't we – I thought your quiz proved it.'

'Mmm, you're right. Starr's just so perfect, that's all. She makes me feel like a *freak*.'

There, I've said it. Not that it's news to Scott, he's heard it all before. I'm always moaning about my looks.

'Maddy, don't say that! You're *not* a freak. But if you really feel that bad, maybe I will give her a call and—'

'No! Forget I said it, Scott. I'm just being stupid, I know I am.'

It's true – after all that sensible advice I've read from Lifecoach Laura in my mags, here I am acting like an idiot.

'The fashion show's important – well, raising money for charity is, anyway. You're right, it's good that Starr's helping us. Come on, let's go.'

♥ ★ ♡

When we get off the bus and walk into the centre of town I can see that *The Dirty Rascal* has had a complete makeover.

(Mad's note: More like cosmetic surgery!)

There's an eye-catching red and black sign saying

Bar Salsa and huge floor-to-ceiling windows reflecting on to the street like celebrity sunglasses.

We stand for a moment peering in like fans at a film-set.

It's Sunday afternoon and the place is empty – all light, space and shiny surfaces. There's a gleaming chrome counter with high bar stools and lots of exotic signs – *Cuban Cocktails*, *Spicy Mexican Snacks* and *Costa Rica Coffees*.

It's a bit of a contrast to the cosy, central-heated, little house I've just left behind. Do real people actually live here?

'Starr said we could press the bell on the main door,' Scott says, hesitating. 'Or d'you think we'd better look for a side-entrance?'

Brrringgggg!

My finger's on the buzzer before he can make a move. Last time I saw a scene like this it was between the pages of a glossy magazine. Now's our chance to get the inside story!

'Hello?' Starr's voice whispers huskily through the air.

'Scott and Maddy for the charity show meeting,' Scott says to the intercom. 'Can we get in this way?'

The door buzzes. 'Come in and make yourself at home. I'm on my way down.'

I push the door and it's like we've just stepped on to the set of a photo-shoot for *Vogue*. Our feet tap across the polished floor and we sink down into a squashy leather sofa.

In front of us is a chrome and marble staircase. No doubt Starr will make her model-girl entrance down it. I wonder what she looks like out of school uniform? I can see her right now, posing in her high heels, designer clothes and make-up...

So you found it all right then?' Starr's voice interrupts me as she appears from a door behind the bar.

She's wearing scruffy jeans, a ripped, black T-shirt and her hair's tied up in a black band. She's barefoot and barefaced – not a designer label in sight – but somehow she still manages to look perfect.

Your mate looks great!

Do you tell the truth and compliment her – or let loose with your cattiest comment ever?

'Oops, sorry Starr, I think we're a bit early. You're obviously not ready yet. Don't worry, we can wait while you get changed,' I say, like some catty fashion critic.

What's going on – I didn't mean to say that! And who am I to talk anyway?

Luckily Starr just laughs. 'I must look a total mess! I was just upstairs practising some salsa – you have to wear baggy, old clothes so you can move freely. I'll show you the dance room on the way up. Matt and Honey are out at the warehouse now so we've got the place to ourselves.'

The dance room is amazing – like a wall-to-wall hall of mirrors. Starr puts on some hot Latino music.

'I thought we could teach the models some basic salsa moves to loosen them up so they move well on the catwalk', she says. 'The mirrors help you check out your body from all angles,' she adds as she sees the look of horror on my face.

(Mad's note: I'm mirror-phobic. In the world-of-Maddy they'd all be banned!)

Then she holds out her hands and starts wiggling her hips to the music. 'D'you want a go? Maddy? Scott? Just copy me OK? One, two, three – tap! Five, six, seven – tap!'

Starr makes it look so easy and the music is so catchy that I forget myself and start joining in with her. Even Scott gets up to dance, too, which is a first.

I'm just getting in the groove when I look up and get an eyeful of myself reflected a thousand times in the mirrors...

Cringerama!! I'm like the freaky fat lady at the funfair! All my humps, bumps and lady lumps look twice the size they used to be – they're shaking in the back and in the front...and at either side, too! I sit down on the floor double-quick and then bum-shuffle back to the wall.

Scott comes over. 'Everything OK?'

'Just-need-to-catch-my-breath' I say quickly. 'Let me watch for a bit so I can see how it looks.'

'One, two, three – tap! Five, six, seven – tap!' Starr counts him in and I try not to laugh. Compared to Starr, Scott looks like a rusty robot.

But Starr does her best. 'That's it! You've got the basics. Now you just need to loosen your hips a bit and listen to the rhythm. Try this...'

She stands in front of Scott and puts her hand in his. Then she tells him to put his hand on what she calls 'the small of her back'.

I stop laughing.

Small of her back?

Hah!

Why doesn't she just come out with it and say, *Feel my hump, honey, mmm, nice!*

Oops! Did I just think that? It's happening again, I keep hearing this voice like I'm possessed or something. Whatever would sensible Lifecoach Laura say?

She'd tell me to take a deep breath and get a grip. It's only a dance, after all...

'Right, the man leads,' Starr continues. 'You go forward and I go back. Wait for the beat and...one, two, three – tap! Five, six, seven – tap!'

And now their moves are flowing, their hips are swaying and my cheeks are flaming...

Am I jealous?

No-no-no-no-NO. Definitely not.

Your mate's found a new friend.

Do you welcome her into your group – the more the merrier? Or do you scratch out her eyes with your sharpened claws?

Skreeeeeeeeeeek!

There's a sound like a strangled cat when I bang on the CD player with my fist and the lid flies open. In the sudden silence Scott and Starr separate, shocked and breathless.

'Sorry, sorry...my hand must have slipped or something – I really didn't *mean* to hit it so hard,' I say, waving my hands around and blushing.

Scott tucks his shirt back tightly into his jeans.

'A-hem never mind, we ought to stop now, anyway. We've got a schedule to work out.'

He checks his watch and shrugs his shoulders at Starr. 'Better get on with it. Anyway, Maddy's the model – not me. She should have been up here dancing.'

'You've done that before, though, haven't you?' Starr says as she leads the way out.

Scott grins. 'Hmm, yeah well I've done my share of windin' and grindin' at family parties. My granny taught me a thing or two...'

I stare at him like I've never seen him before.

Buttoned-up Scott winding and grinding? He's my best friend and yet there are things I never knew about him till now.

Do I really know Scott as well as I think I do?

And what other little secrets is he going to tell Starr?

Zero points – You FAILED the envy exam!

Lifecoach Laura says, 'You ARE a jealousy junkie! You're in a mean, green place and you're feeding off your fears. Stop now – or an overdose of jealousy will end in tears...'

6

PROBLEM PAGE

Scott and Starr are sorting stuff out about the fashion show now, but I'm not really listening. I'm thinking about what Scott said when he stopped dancing. He said, *Maddy's the model, not me.*

Does he know something that I don't know?

Has he put my name down for the show?

Panic Attack! I'm desperate to ask him but there's no way I'm doing it in front of Starr. A perfect supermodel like her couldn't possibly understand my hall-of-mirrors, bouncy-bumps trauma, but Scott might. He can be very sensitive sometimes... for a boy.

They're still talking plans and dates but it's life-crisis time and I can't cope with such minor details.

I take a look around the flat to calm my tortured nerves but that just make things worse. Even up here everything looks shiny and perfect like a brand new magazine still in its wrapper. Not like my place – *lived-in*, Mum calls it. I call it a mess.

Starr's so lucky. No clutter from pesky parents and no brat of a brother to make it smelly and scruffy. She hasn't even got a dog either, so no muddy paw-prints, or bones buried under the sofa...

(Mad's note: Yes, I know a handbag-sized pooch is the latest designer accessory but my dog, Chester – an overweight mongrel – definitely doesn't count.)

A burst of salsa music suddenly blasts up from downstairs. It's so loud I can feel the floorboards vibrating under us but Starr doesn't seem at all surprised.

'Matt and Honey must be back,' she says, yawning and stretching. 'They're practising for the free class they're giving tonight to launch *Red Hot Salsa Sundays*... sorry about the noise.'

'Don't worry, we've got everything sorted anyway. Time to go,' Scott says standing up.

I stand up, too. I can't wait to see Starr's glam parents after all we've heard about them.

'I'll show you out down the back stairs,' Starr says, raising her voice over the throbbing music. 'Best not to disturb Honey before a big night. Things are a bit tense at the moment. She really wants these salsa nights to take off.'

So I go downstairs feeling cheated out of a chance to zoom in on Starr's production team. But as soon as we're out of the door I remember my life-crisis and grab Scott's arm.

'If you say yes to my next question, then I'm dead,' I say, staring deep into his eyes.

He looks deeply back. He can tell I'm serious. 'Oh no! You heard about the magazine strike already? Sorry—'

'Fun-*nee*. Worse than that. Did you put my name down to be a model? Tell me now. My life depends on it!'

'Well, what if I did? It's your magazine-dream, isn't it?'

'Nooo! You didn't? How could you? Say you're joking – please.'

'*You're joking, please.*'

'Scott!'

And now he puts on his serious class-rep face and says, 'Listen up, Maddy. I swear on my mother's life I did not put your name down as a model. I thought you did. It's what you want, isn't it?'

'No! The dream's turned into a nightmare – especially after I caught sight of my lady lumps in those mirrors when we were dancing.'

'Er...lady lumps?'

'Yeah, well let's put it this way. I've got lumps, bumps

and camel humps and they're not all where they should be either. I'm not parading them on stage for everyone to laugh at.'

'Maddy, you're just...curvy. My mum always says it's a good thing for a girl to have some flesh on her bones.'

'Why? What are they gonna do at this fashion show? Watch us or eat us? No, my mind's made up. I'm not doing it.'

'OK, if that's what you want. No one's forcing you.'

'Thanks – if anyone found out I wanted to be a model I'd die of shame! Don't tell anyone, will you, Scott? It's our secret, right?'

'Cross my heart, hope to die, stick a needle in my eye,' he says, miming the actions.

'Yeah, well you don't have to go that far, Lord Nelson. But thanks – you're a pal', I say, linking his arm as we start walking again.

'Of course that doesn't mean I don't think you'd look good on the catwalk. In fact I think you'd look really—'

'Shut up now, OK? Or you'll lose the other eye.'

So, next day, I'm feeling sad but noble when Miss Bruce gets ready to read out the model names.

Yes, it's true – if Starr hadn't come to our school then perhaps I'd have given the model-girl-thing a whirl. But hey, it's not her fault she's blonde, beautiful and only bounces in all the right places, is it?

No. We all have our faults and I forgive her. I'll even

say 'Congratulations!' when her name's read out.

'Now, let's see which volunteers are brave enough to get on stage for Scott's charity,' Miss Bruce says. She opens the box and starts to unfold scraps of paper. 'So the fashion show models are...number one: Ashley Lewis...number two: Maddy Blue... number three—'

Shock Horror!! Double-page nightmare to cut out and keep!

I don't even hear the rest of the names.

I don't hear anything.

My head starts buzzing like an instant sugar-rush, but I can guess what everyone's saying. *Maddy Blue – a model? That's a laugh. Who does she think she is?*

Did Scott lie to me? I look round but he's distracted by Starr who's whispering in his ear. Then everyone piles out of class but I can't move.

'Time to go home,' Scott says, standing over me. 'Come on model Maddy – I knew you'd put your name down in the end.'

'What? I didn't – it was you!' I say, finding my voice at last.

'No, I—'

'It was me,' Starr says smiling. Then she sees my face and adds, 'Isn't that what you wanted? When you came up with the fashion show idea, I thought you'd like to try but you seemed a bit shy...'

I'm not listening. Now I get it – the classic problem page scenario.

Only this time it's not on the page, it's for real...

My best friend blabbed my secret! **TRUST OR BUST?**

Three's a crowd. *BETRAYED BY A MATE!*

'Scott, you told her,' I say and my voice is a shocked whisper. 'You promised you wouldn't tell anyone... It was our secret and you told her.'

'Maddy, I—'

But I'm scrambling out of my chair and everything's a blur of tears and anger.

Can an old friendship stand the test?

My face is hot and that voice in my head starts speaking for me. Words are tumbling out of my mouth that I didn't even know were there till now.

'I trusted you... I thought we were best friends but you blabbed my secret, didn't you? Nothing's been the same since she got here.'

I'm jabbing a finger at Starr but Scott folds his hand around mine.

'Maddy, you've got it all wrong. You're overreacting! Let's get out of school and—'

'No! Leave me alone, will you?' I shake him off and stalk to the door.

'How can I trust you now? Whose friend are you – mine or Starr's?'

They're both staring at me open-mouthed but I don't wait for an answer.

'And you can forget about your stupid fashion show. Find someone else to act the fool. I quit!'

7

CONTACT US

Bad Day?

NOBODY LOVES YOU?

Can your life get any worse?

DON'T FORGET!
YOU'RE NOT ALONE...

I wish I could edit out the last page but I can't.

By the time I walk home I regret every word and I feel terrible.

What's happening to me? I used to be a nice, quiet person but now I've turned into the *hysterical mag-hag from hell.*

I'M SO CONFUSED!

All I want to do now is close the door to my room, lie on my bed, have a good cry and *never ever* come out again.

But Fate is against me and my misery – there are happy omens bobbing about on the front door handle...

Three blue balloons.

No! It's Max's birthday party. He went on and on about being three this morning...how could I forget?

As soon as I step inside our house it's total kiddy kaos.

(Mad's note: It's CHAOS: kan't you spell?)

At least a hundred mini spidermen, batmen and supermen are diving down stairs, swinging from lampshades and staging intergalactic battles from behind random bits of furniture.

I HATE MY LIFE!

Then Mum comes fussing over to me and for some reason she's carrying a giant, green bogey on a plate.

'Hi Maddy love, look! I saved you a nice, big slice of Max's superhero cake. Now don't be put off by the bright green icing it's really very—'

'*Mmph*...not hungry,' I mutter.

The battle troups re-group and I spy an escape route opening up ahead. At last I reach the safety of my room, close the door and wedge a chair against it to keep it shut. Now for that Good Cry.

I slump on to my bed and manage a sniffle or two. Then a warm wet tongue splats my face and a wave of dog breath washes over me.

'Go away, Chester!' I snivel, pushing at him half-heartedly.

He wags his tail and moves in closer. This passes for affection in his strange doggy world. Of course, I end up stroking him and even though I still want to cry, I can't. I just feel sad and empty.

So I do what I always do every evening after school – find my phone, search for Scott's number and...

And what?

What am I going to do?

Call him up and say, 'Ooh, you'll never guess what – I've just had a big bust-up with someone at school today! ... Who? ... Oh, yeah – it's *you*.'

I throw the phone down on my bed and a solitary tear trickles down my cheek.

As if Scott would ever want to talk to me again after my *Double-Diva De-luxe* performance today!

Even if he didn't like Starr better than me before, he certainly will now.

Someone's sticking red hot needles into the back of my eyeballs and the room's getting all blurry. At least now I can have that Big Cry. I'm gulping air and my shoulders start to heave when—

'Maddy!' Mum's knocking at the door. 'It's all about me!'

'(*Gulp.*) What's (*gulp*) all about you?' I shout back – I've found it's best not to ignore her, she only gets hysterical. Must be her age.

'No love, I mean your magazine *It's All About Me.* It came today and I thought you'd like to read it.'

I open the door a crack and she pokes it through the gap.

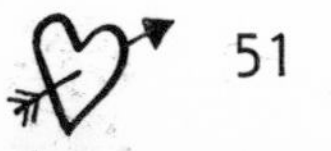

'Everything all right?' she says, trying to prise the door open a bit more.

'Perfect!' I snap, slamming it shut again and wedging it tight.

Then I look at my magazine and my eyes clear. I stroke the bright, shiny cover and the sun comes out...

(*Mad's note: You mean you switch the light on to see better.*)

And when I flick through the pages and skim the headings it's like my best friend just walked in the room.

Fun! FASHION! Features! *Photos!*

QUIZZES! CRUSHES! Cringes! Advice!

Someone I've known for ages, someone who understands me, someone I can talk to...

FRIENDSHIP FALL-OUTS? BOYFRIEND BLUES? BODY PROBLEMS?

Don't sit in your room and suffer alone...
Our panel of trained teen-trauma experts are here to help you.
We'll dry your tears and fix your fears.

Contact: It's All About Me™ **and do it now!**

I pick up my pen and start writing,

Dear It's All About Me,
You're the only friend I've got left in
the whole world. My best friend (make
that ex-best friend) blabbed my most
embarrassing secret. At least I think he did.
He denied it but I went mad at him
anyway. Now I'm so confused.
He said I overreacted but nothing's the
same any more. Ever since this new girl joined
our gang I knew things would go wrong.
Now I'm all alone. What can I do?
M. B.
(Miserable and Blue)

I feel a bit better after splurging it on to paper. Peace has broken out in the house, too. It's Kiddie Kurfew time and the battle troops have been dragged off home.

Mum's giving Max a bath and Dad's watching TV so no one bothers me as I grab a stamp from downstairs. Then I make a dash for the postbox at the end of our street.

Typical! I missed the last collection by five minutes. Never mind, it'll go first thing in the morning.

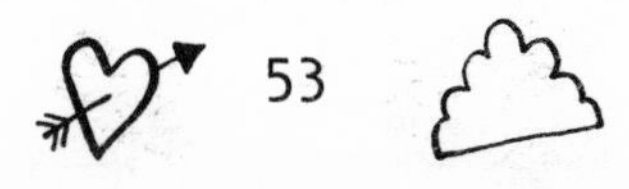

But what if the postbox is attacked by a gang of masked raiders in the night and my letter ends up as litter?

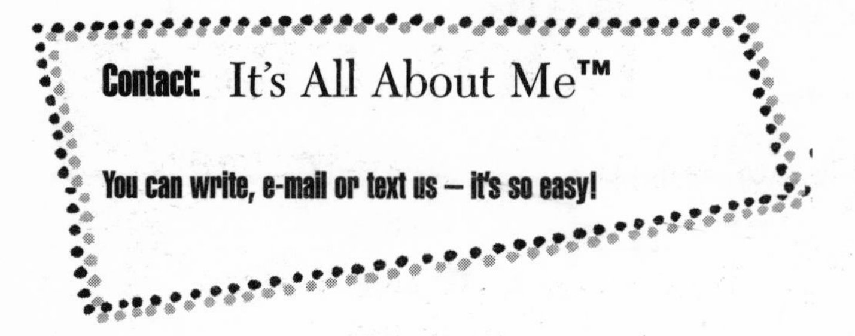

I go home, type up the problem and then send it to *It's All About Me* as an e-mail.

But what if my computer's got a vicious virus that infects my mail so it lies around in cyberspace going nowhere fast?

I get out my phone and
txt the prblm 1x
2x
Well 3x, jst to b safe.

8

FEEL GOOD – LOOK GREAT!

Beat stress with our 7 Steps to Happiness!

1 Take time off your daily routine and have some ME time.

Next day I wake up feeling terrible. I can't possibly go to school.

No, honest. It's nothing to do with having to face Scott and Starr hanging out together while I sit on my own like a total saddo. I am definitely ill.

'I'm really hot,' I say to Mum when she storms into my room next morning to see why I'm not up. 'It must be a virus.'

'I bet you caught it from one of those computers,' she says, feeling my forehead. 'They say you can pick up all sorts of bugs from them.'

'Tell me that's a joke', I say, feebly.

I'll never know the answer to that question. She just looks at me thoughtfully and says, 'Well you don't feel very hot.'

'N...now I'm f...freezing cold,' I winge, my teeth chattering uncontrollably. 'That's w...worse isn't it? Hot and c...cold flushes? Maybe it's f...flu? Or f...food poisoning?'

'Food poisoning? Have you eaten anything that didn't agree with you?'

'Only that p...party cake you f...force-fed me late last night. It tasted like—'

'Oh dear, I hope it's not that. All the boys at the party had cake – and Max had second helpings...'

She looks worried for a nano-second until Max bounces in, followed by Chester. Then he jumps on my bed and growls (Max, not the dog – he's too fat and flops on the floor.)

'Geroff, me. Maddy's ill!' I say turning my face to the wall.

Woof! That's Max again. He's having one of his I-am-a-dog days. It was quite cute the first time. Then it got *really* annoying. He wouldn't stop sniffing, barking and growling, even when I had friends round.

Friend, that is.

Scott.

My ex-friend.

Maddy no-mates. That's me.

'Feel awful,' I mumble, pulling the duvet over my head.

Mum sighs. 'I think you're a bit run down. You'd better

stay in bed today and we'll see how you feel tomorrow. I've got to take Max to nursery now.'

Woof!'

'Won't be long. D'you want me to pick something up from the shop on the way back?'

I poke my nose out from under the duvet, 'Magazines, please... *EEeuw – MUM!* Max just licked my face!'

'That boy needs a muzzle,' she mutters on her way out.

2 Find something you like doing and throw yourself into it. A new hobby might lead to new friends...

The rest of the day is a total mag-fest. Who needs Scott and Starr anyway? I'm having a party and I'm in good company. Mum's bought me a pic 'n' mix selection of magazines and I spread them out on the bed scanning the happy headings.

WANT IT? WIN IT! **Eat yourself happy!** **FIVE FLIRTY**

Be a cutie beauty! **Max your life!** **POCKET PIN-UPS!**

I enter competitions, do quizzes, follow flow charts, read top tips, lust after lads, check out the problem pages and browse the best buys.

I feel *fab-tastic* already!

Well, I will do after I've taken my *Seven Steps to Happiness* – then maybe I won't feel so sad any more...

3 Drink lots of water, it's free!
(or try Gulp! Great bottled water for girls on the go!)

4 Shine your hair in seconds with our free wax conditioner
(for best results leave on for two hours)

5 Smooth your skin with our Seaweed and Sandpaper face pack
(not suitable for sensitive skin types)

6 Brighten up your bath with our free Nettle and Dandelion bath bomb
(from the new 'Weeds are Flowers, too' range)

7 Do a Yoga for Young People work-out!
Copy our model on page 63
(new TV series starts next week)

So while Mum's out in the afternoon collecting Max from nursery I have a home-health spa session. I run a bath, throw in a fizzy bath-bomb (strange smell but, *hey* – that's nature for you!), apply the wax to my hair and wrap it in a towel, lay back and relax – *aahhh!*

A happy half hour later I get out, drink the

recommended eight glasses of water (feel a bit sick, but never mind – it's good for me) and smooth on the face-pack (minty smell but same bogey-green as Max's birthday cake.)

Then I pull on some jogging pants, a big baggy T-shirt and start the yoga work-out.

The hardest move is the shoulder stand. I cheat a bit and lie down with my bum squashed against the bedroom wall. Then I start sort of backward-climbing up it until my legs are stretched up high and...

At last – I'm upside down!

Ooo-err! The blood rushes from my feet to my face pack and all that water sloshes around in my stomach.

I feel sick and dizzy but if I do this for a minute I'll be happy. The mag says so.

I close my eyes and start counting, *1, 2, 3, 4, 5, 6*—

'Maddy, you've got a visitor!'

The door bursts open and Mum barges in, totally ignoring my *Please Knock – Puberty in Progress* poster.

'I told him you were ill but I think the company will do you good. Come in, Scott, while I get you both a drink.'

Pleease! This cannot be happening to me! Maybe if I keep my eyes closed it will all turn out to be a dream?

(Mad's note: Correction - nightmare. Top score on the blush-ometer.)

Then I hear a familiar voice, 'Er, sorry Maddy. This obviously isn't a good time for you, I'd better go.'

'Mmpgh,' I say, cracking my face pack into a thousand scribbles.

Then I slide sideways down the wall, scramble to my feet and pull my T-shirt down from round my neck. *Major cringe or what?*

'Sorry, I didn't catch what you said,' he says looking at me with concern. 'Are you all right?'

'Not really,' I say scattering green flakes all over the carpet.

But I don't care. It's so good to see Scott that, for once, I forget about how I look.

I forget about everything except Lifecoach Laura and her top tip to use after an argument.

'Scott, about yesterday. Can we talk things through d'you think?'

'I hope so.' He sits down on the edge of the bed.

It's only been a day but I've definitely missed him. Maybe one day with Starr has made him realise how much he's missed me, too?

OK, take a deep breath, I tell myself. Try to sound calm, mature and sensible, just like Lifecoach Laura herself. I bet we can be best friends again if I can just find the right words...

'Scott, I... *Eek!* – need a big wee!'

I dash to the door – nearly trip over Max in the hall – and stumble to the bathroom just in time...

(Mad's note: Water Warning! Excess H_2O intake can cause embarrassing side effects. Drink in moderation and remain upright for at least fifteen minutes afterwards.)

9

FRIENDSHIP FIRST AID

One minute you're best mates – the next you're worst enemies. What happened? All friendships have their break-ups but it doesn't have to be terminal!

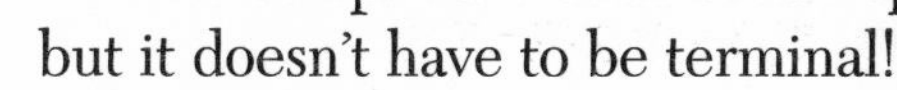

USE LIFECOACH LAURA'S

FOR A QUICK FIX…

'I'm so relieved,' I say to Scott a few minutes later. He's sitting on my bed reading one of the millions of magazines scattered all over the room.

'Most people are, after a trip to the loo,' he says, without looking up.

'No, I mean relieved that you're still here. I thought you might have gone… I wouldn't blame you after I lost my temper yesterday.'

'What happened, Maddy? That wasn't like you! It was scary.'

'I *know*. Hissy fit, or what? I suppose I was just hurt because you—'

He looks up sharply, 'Maddy, I did not tell Starr you wanted to be a model. You're my best friend and I gave you my word. Do you really think I'd go back on it?'

He gives me a full-on, front-cover, mag-model stare.

I feel bad and look away.

1 Apply a Sticking Plaster

If you've made a mistake, take a deep breath and say 'Sorry'.
It's a small word but it'll make you both feel a whole lot better!

'Scott I'm sorry... When Miss Bruce read my name out I just flipped. I didn't know what to think. And why did Starr have to put my name down anyway? What's it got to do with her?'

'Like she said, she thought it was what you'd want. She was trying to make you happy! Even if she got it wrong, did you have to sound off like that? Why couldn't you talk about it calmly? Like you are now.'

'Dunno what happened. I just saw red, I suppose...'

'Or green?'

'Green? What's that supposed to mean?'

Then I catch sight of myself in the mirror. 'Ooops – the face pack!' My hands fly to my face and I touch my flaky green skin. 'I should have washed it off ten minutes ago! Back in a sec. Don't go away...'

This time I tread carefully out into the hall but there's no puppy-dog Max around. He must be in his kennel or something.

Mum's bustling up the stairs with drinks but I dodge into the bathroom before she starts chatting and my face turns to concrete.

2 *Examine the symptoms carefully.*

What went wrong? Listen to what your friend says and try to see things from their point of view.
The results might surprise you!

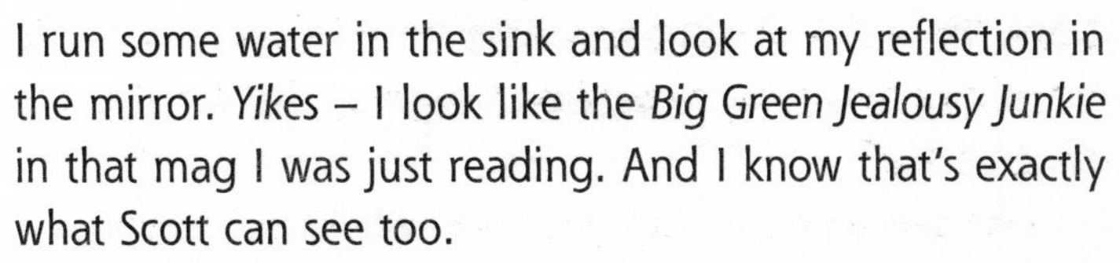

I run some water in the sink and look at my reflection in the mirror. *Yikes* – I look like the *Big Green Jealousy Junkie* in that mag I was just reading. And I know that's exactly what Scott can see too.

I splash warm water on my face and try to wash the thought away.

Jealousy Junkie? – Me?

No, I've read every article, quiz and problem page on the subject that's ever been written. I know everything there is to know about the problems and pitfalls of jealousy. He's got it all wrong.

'Nearly normal,' I say going back into my room. 'Face-pack gone, anyway.'

Scott hands me a mug of tea. 'Are you sure?'

I touch my face with my fingers. 'Have I missed a bit? Am I still green?' I groan.

'Maddy, you look fine.' He sighs, 'But that's not what I meant and you know it. Listen, what have you got against Starr? As far as I can see she's just trying to be your friend and—'

'*Your* friend, you mean. Anyway, what could I possibly have against Starr? Just because she's got a posh flat, glam parents and model girl looks... What's there to be jealous of?'

Scott doesn't say a word. He doesn't have to.

Even I have to admit that didn't sound too convincing. But I'm not ready to take all the blame.

'I have *tried,* Scott. Remember that friendship flow chart – I was trying to find out where she fitted in but *you* interrupted me before I had time to finish.'

'Maddy, I did that deliberately. I could see she was struggling to answer the question about what she normally does when she hangs out with her friends.'

'Was she...why?'

'Because she'd just finished telling us how she moved around all the time. So she's not exactly going to have loads of friends to hang out with, is she?'

'Oh...maybe not.' I'm a bit taken aback at this. You don't really expect *Beautiful People* to have the same problems as the rest of us, do you? I sort of assumed that if you look perfect, then your life is perfect, too, isn't it?

'OK, so I got her all wrong but she got me wrong, too.

I don't want to be a model in the show. Especially if *she's* going to be one...'

'She's not. She didn't put her name down because she wants to customise the clothes instead.'

'Does she?'

It's *Surprise Central* in here today. Why doesn't Starr want to be a model? She's born to it. It's in her genes.

(Mad's note: or jeans...)

Now I'm starting to feel like a complete idiot.

'*Omigod.* You must hate me, Scott – and Starr, too. What am I like? I got everything wrong and I was so horrible to you – and her. Now I've ruined everything and—'

'Whoa. Stop right there, drama diva. Don't start overreacting again! Let's forget it. We're friends for life, remember?'

I nod.

'So, d'you think we can get back on track? We've got to – I need my dream team for the show. Will you be well enough to go to school tomorrow?'

I sniff pathetically (*sniff*), 'Yeah,' (*cough*) 'I think so. But what am I going to say to Starr?'

'Don't worry about it.' Scott stands up.

Then he sits down again and starts flicking through one of my mags. 'Um, Maddy, I've been thinking... About me helping Starr settle in, showing her around and everything. Did that make you feet a bit *left out?*'

'S'pose so,' I shrug. 'Where'd you get that flash of inspiration from all of a sudden?'

Scott picks a mag up off the bed and passes it to me.

'I read it while you were in the bathroom. Look – *Two's company, is Three a Crowd?* It's a very interesting article. You should read these magazines some time... Lifecoach Laura's got some very good advice... *Oww!*'

I roll up the mag and start hitting him with it.

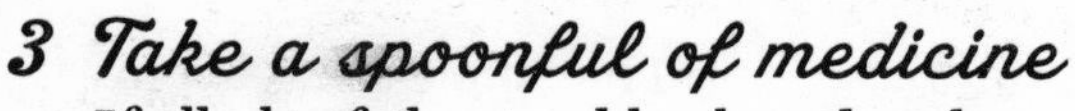

3 *Take a spoonful of medicine*

If all else fails, stand back and make a joke out of it.
Laughter's the best form of medicine, after all!

(Mad's note: We're talking friendship first aid here, not actual fractures. In case of broken bones consult a doctor IMMEDIATELY.)

10

SHOP TILL YOU DROP

WHAT EVERY GIRL WANTS

Sometimes you just want to chill out and have fun with your friends. Why not try a girly day out and shop till you drop...

'Scott, I can't do it. How can I face Starr after what I said? She's going to hate me, I know it.'

I'm standing at the school gates feeling sick.

Saying sorry to Starr all sounded so easy when we were skimming through the sensible advice pages in the magazines.

Now that it's a reality I'd rather salsa stark naked on a celebrity TV dance show.

'Maddy, there's nothing to worry about. Think of what your magazines said – just take a deep breath and be honest. That's all it takes.'

'OK, deep breath. Honest. Deep breath...' I stagger

through the school gates and along the corridor towards our class.

Scott opens the door and waits for me to go in but I dodge past him. 'Bathroom,' I mouth, flapping my hands like a pair of wet face-cloths, 'it's a lady thing...'

It's also a lie, of course, and Scott knows it – but where I'm going he can't follow...

So I stay locked up in the loo till the bell goes for the first lesson. Then I sneak into class at the last minute to avoid any chance that Starr and I might have of talking.

Who knows, if I can keep this up for a whole year, she might even forget I exist—

Just as I'm thinking this a note lands on my desk.

Luckily the teacher's a bit distracted at the moment because there's a wasp buzzing around at the windows and half the class is hysterical (mainly the boys).

I open the note and read.

Dear Maddy,

I don't blame you for avoiding me after what I did the other day. It was wrong to put your name forward as a model without asking you.

Please believe me when I say SORRY!!

You and Scott were so good to me when I started here that I wanted to do something to make you feel good, too. I saw you looking at the fashion pages in magazines and thought you'd enjoy being in the show.

Sorry if I got it wrong. Can we be friends?

Starr

Now I feel even worse.

Starr's done what I should have – she's said sorry. Ooh she's so perfect – I hate her! No I don't. What am I saying? She's a wonderful person – I *like* her. Of course I do – who wouldn't?

I look up from the note and catch her watching me. Her face is one big question mark.

I smile and she smiles back.

Just like that, we're friends again.

So what do we do now?

It's Saturday morning and I'm meeting up with Starr first thing. I don't know what to wear – I mean, what do girls wear on shopping trips?

The only shopping Scott and I do is on the way home from school when we call into the newsagent's (for my mags). But this is different – Sergeant Scott's given us orders to buy clothes for the fashion show while he sorts out the sound and lighting 'on set' as he calls it.

So this really is serious shopping like I've read about in my mags! Maybe I should dress up and wear something pink and sparkly?

No, I decide against it due to the fact that,

a. I don't have anything pink and sparkly
b. I don't have anything pink and sparkly
c. See above

Starr and I are meeting outside *Bar Salsa*. I get off the bus and she's already waiting. She's gone for the casual look again – jeans and T-shirt – but she still looks so *superstarry* – like she's posing for a 'Girl's Day Out' mag feature.

Guess what? Her t-shirt's pink and sparkly.

Why is it that when Starr wears pink and sparkly she doesn't look air-head girly – she looks *ironic*. If I wore that T-shirt I'd look *moronic*.

How does she do that?

'Hi Maddy!'

'Hi Starr!'

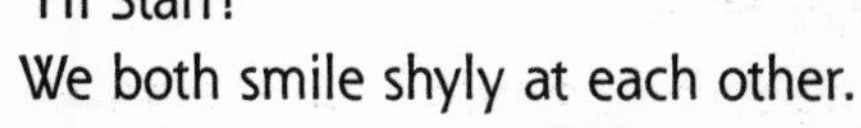

We both smile shyly at each other. Maybe Starr's new to girlie-shopping days, too.

'So, where shall we start our bargain bonanza?' I ask, trying to sound enthusiastic.

'Oh, I'm...not sure. Are there many charity shops in town?'

'Yeah, my mum has been known to drag me along to some on the High Street. Shall we start there?' I say.

'OK.'

We both stand as still as shop-window dummies till Starr says, 'Um... I don't really know where the High Street is...'

'Oh, right. Follow me.'

It's funny, Starr's lived in another country and she knows a big city like London but she seems so helpless all of a sudden.

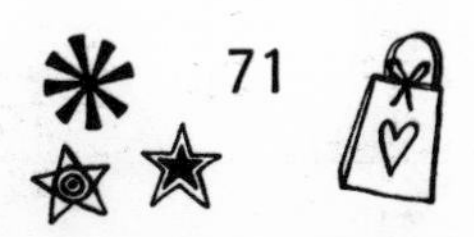

I can't imagine not knowing every stone of boring, small-town Westfield and decide to give her the benefit of my wisdom.

'OK, here we are on the world-famous Westfield High Street. It's got fabulous designer shops and fantastic department stores. Ooh, look – *Nearly New, Next to Nothing, Cheap 'n' Cheerful and Everything Must Go* – classy!'

Starr heads straight into *Nearly New*. I only hope she's got better taste than my mum – she always buys me big woolly jumpers in the middle of summer just 'cos they're in the bargain-bin.

Luckily Starr seems to have a built-in style radar. All I can see is cheap tat and rubbish but she picks out skirts, shirts, belts and scarves which look like they've got possibilities.

'Once we've got the basics we can customise them how we want,' she says. 'It's an autumn show so the key colours

to look out for are olive greens, burnt oranges, dark plums and rich wines.'

My mouth starts to water – she sounds more like a top chef than a style guru. 'You mean red and purple?' I say, going over to a colour co-ordinated clothes rack and rattling a few hangers like I know what I'm doing.

'Huh? Hmm, yes, but we'll need to contrast the dark colours with bright accessories. Look for bronze, silver and gold.

'Ok.' I hand over a slinky, scarlet red dress and a pair of big, gold hoop earrings. 'Right, that's the boys sorted. Now what about the girls?'

Starr smiles. 'You're funny, Maddy, You make people laugh. I wish I could do that.'

'Yeah, but you're gonna make people look great. *That's* talent. I can't do that, not even for myself.'

She stops and holds up a wine-coloured top against me. 'I could make you look great,' she says. Then her hand flies up to her mouth. 'Ooh, not that you don't look good now, of course. I mean—'

'Don't worry, I know what you mean,' I say sadly. 'Listen, if I thought I could look good I'd still be a model in the show.'

'Really?' Starr looks strangely happy at that idea. 'You know, that's what I'd like to do when I leave school,' she says dreamily, 'go to art college and become a fashion designer.'

'Yeah – well, why not?'

'Because Honey's got other ideas,' she says. 'But listen,

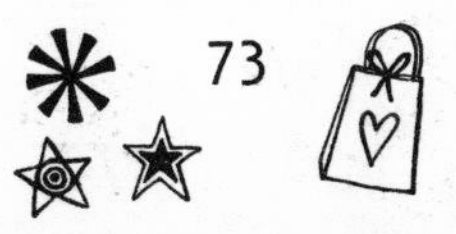

why don't I use you as my first model? We can do a makeover session tonight.'

'Tonight? I'm not sure...'

'Come for a sleepover. Then we can take our time...'

Sleepover, makeover – not the type of thing I do with Scott!

'Ok, I'll ask my mum. I bet she'll say yes. She'll be glad to get rid of me for the night.'

'Cool, Matt and Honey won't mind. They'll be working all evening.'

(Mad's note: Shopping, makeover, sleepover. It's like living in the pages of a teen magazine...)

11

THINGS TO DO ON A SLEEPOVER

- ♥ Paint your nails
- ♥ Try on clothes
- ♥ *Listen to your fave music*
- ♥ TALK ABOUT BOYS
- ♥ Eat tasty treats
- ♥ **Style each other's hair**

That's what my mag says but I've never done stuff like this before. Yes, I like to read my girlie-mags but until I met Starr that's all I did.

Now it's like I'm stepping into girl-world and I'm not sure if it's really for me. I feel like a fake and I bet Starr will soon see through my act...

The bus is nearly at my stop now, so I put the mag away. It's only a short walk to the side door of *Bar Salsa* and I'm feeling more and more nervous. Maybe I'll make some excuse and tell Starr I can't do the sleepover after all. I press the bell.

Brrringgg!!

When the door opens I'm so surprised at what I see that I'm stunned into silence.

'*Hola chica* – you must be Maddy! Starr's told me all about you. Come in and I'll get her for you. Don't mind me, I'm glamming up for tonight. It takes me longer and longer to put my face on these days!'

Starr's mum looks like her big sister. She's blonde and tanned but she doesn't dress like Starr. She's wearing high-heeled strappy sandals, fishnets and a slinky, silky dressing gown. Half of her hair is in jumbo rollers and the other half tumbles over her shoulders like Starr's. Her eyes are made up with eye-liner and smoky dark eyeshadow and her lips are pale.

She looks *soooo glammy* – like a celebrity getting ready for a Saturday-night show. I didn't know mums could look like that. My mum just looks ordinary.

She's chatting again as she leads the way upstairs. 'It's so cool for Starr to have a friend here. She hasn't always found it easy to fit in at her other schools. Lot of jealousy, you know? Girls can be very cruel sometimes. I learned that in my modelling days... Starr – you've got a visitor!'

We're on the top floor now and Starr appears from her room. There's a sign on the door with her name and a border of stars around it like she's in the movies or something.

'Right, I'll love you and leave you. If you want some food you've only got to phone down. It's salsa night so everything's extra hot and spicy!'

'Cheers.'

'Keep your fingers crossed for me, Starr. I really want this evening to work out! If we can get ten couples for the salsa nights they could really take off. Then we can have special weekends and people from other cities coming for dance nights. Anything to put some life into this dump—'

'Honey!'

'Oh, sorry love. But Westfield's not exactly London or Madrid is it? If you'd told me at your age I'd end up here well...let's just put it this way, I had other plans. That's why I don't want you to waste your assets, Starr. Give it another year and we'll contact an agency. I'm really glad you're both working on this fashion show—'

'Maddy's going on the catwalk, not me. I'm designing the clothes, remember?'

'It's not that easy to make it in fashion design, babe. Money talks and if you've got a name – even better. I can see you modelling first and *then* having your own line of clothing – *Reach for the Stars in Starr Fashions!*'

She puts her hand on Starr's cheek. 'Use what nature gave you, OK? You've got the looks and you're still growing. You'll be taller than me, soon. You're catwalk material, not just a glamour model like me. You could really go somewhere. You don't want to spend your life watching every penny, do you?'

Starr shakes her head and brushes her hand away. 'It's only a school fashion show. Don't get carried away!'

Honey looks over at me and sighs, 'Maddy, see if you can talk some sense into her, will you?'

And she swirls away in a silky twirl leaving a trail of perfume.

'*Soo* embarrassing,' Starr says, raising her eyes.

'You think so? I think she's pretty amazing,' I say. 'At least she can see beyond the end of her street. My mum and dad don't care what I do in life – "As long as you're happy, that's all we want." But what is happy? Being like them? Sometimes I just look at them and think – so when did you decide to be *dull*? When did you opt to be *ordinary*?'

Starr's laughing. 'OK, let's forget about them. From now on this is a parent-free zone! Time for some fun!'

THINGS TO DO ON A SLEEPOVER

Have a fashion-show with your friends!
Create a new look!

'Can we do the fashion show later?' I ask when Starr suggests it. 'What about phoning down for that hot 'n' spicy food? Wish I had room service at our house.'

'It gets boring after a while – the menu's a bit limited. Sometimes I just do a potato in the microwave up here. Anyway, we'll sort it later...you can't model on a full stomach! So, what sort of clothes d'you normally wear? What's your style?'

WHAT'S YOUR STYLE?

Funky or Punky?

Sassy or Classy?

Glam or Grunge?

Sporty or Flirty?

'I haven't really got a style. I usually wear black...'

'So you're a bit of a Goth?'

'Um, well not really. It's supposed to be slimming, isn't it? And it doesn't show the dirt much...and it's easy to get more black stuff to match.'

Starr frowns, 'And your hair, d'you always wear it down?'

'Yeah, so it'll hide my face.'

Starr looks at me critcally. 'So you wear your hair and clothes to hide yourself away – sort of like a disguise?'

'Well that's what clothes are for, isn't it? To cover things up – what else?'

Starr opens her star-spangled door.

'Come in, I'll show you...'

Starr's room is a revelation. Guess what? She's a mag-hag like me! There are thousands of thick, glossy magazines piled high in the corner of her room.

'How can you afford these?' I ask, picking up a *Vogue* from the top of the pile.

Starr shrugs. 'Honey buys them for me. Says she's going to see me on the cover one day. In her dreams...'

The walls are covered with fashion pics, too. The only difference is that these models are not so much High Street as High Class. They're style icons, in expensive clothes, who look like they've never pigged-out on chocolate or had a spot in their life!

'How can you live with this lot looking down on you all the time?' I ask Starr. 'At least I can close my mags when I've had enough. Doesn't if make you feel bad?' They're so *perfect*. It's depressing!'

Starr looks around critically, 'Never really thought about it like that.' She moves around the room and then stops and looks at me. 'I didn't put these pictures up just to look at the models, if that's what you think – that's a bit sick!'

'So what did you put them up for?'

'For inspiration – to see how designers mix different looks and create a new style.'

'Yeah?'

'Yes.' She starts moving around the room again like a dancer stepping backwards and forwards. She's pointing at the pictures and reading the words as she moves.

'Look at the clashing styles – **Classic & Crazy, Tailored & Wayward, Military & Madcap**... And I love the weird mix of textures like here – **Leather & Lace, Suede & Brocade, Velvet & Chiffon, Denim & Sequins**—'

'Stop!' I say, covering my ears with my hands. 'You're like some High Priestess of Fashion chanting a spell or something...'

'Am I?' She's laughing now. 'Well, are you under my power yet? Do you want to be transformed?'

'I... I don't know.'

It's strange but after all that time I've spent poring over fashion pages and reading all the beauty advice, now that I've got the chance to join the club, I don't know if I want to.

'It's all a bit vain when you think about it. Decorating yourself up like a Christmas tree. Why? Just to get a boyfriend or something?'

Starr stops laughing. 'Is that what you really think, Maddy?'

'Well, be honest – what else is fashion for?'

12

DO YOU HAVE A PASSION FOR FASHION?

Starr sighs. She sits on her bed and pulls out a huge sketch pad from under it. She opens it up and starts flicking through it.

I can see random drawings and quick sketches of everything and anything – a cat, traffic lights, a face, onion rings, reflections on rooftops, sky.

'Did you do those?' I ask. 'They're really good.'

She nods and passes it over to me. I flick through and see that some of the pages have things pinned to them – a sweet wrapper, a button, a feather, a scrap of material...

'What are these for?'

'Ideas.' Starr says. 'You need to keep a portfolio of sketches and ideas to become a fashion designer. Just like an artist would.'

'I wish I could draw.'

'Well what *are* you good at?

'Pass. Next question?'

'OK, you're funny. So you could show that in your style of dress.'

'Great, I'll buy some clown shoes and a shiny red nose. A definite improvement.'

'Style's all about expressing your personality. Your style could be...witty.'

'I'd rather be pretty.'

'Pretty's bland.'

'Or do you mean blonde? Should I dye my hair?'

'No, it's quite rare to be a natural redhead. I like the colour.'

'You wouldn't say that if you knew the grief I get over it at school – ginger nut, ginger minger, frizzy-lizzy...!'

Try out our hot new hairstyles

If your hair's long and strong, short and sharp, curly and cute – we've got a new look for you!

'Have you tried pinning it up a bit? Starr finds some clips and starts fiddling around with my hair. I go along with her for the laugh. At least I can take it all down before anyone else sees me.

'And all that black makes you look a bit washed out. Let's bin the black and work out what colours suit you best... Here try these...'

She starts rummaging around in the carrier bags from today's shopping trip and lays out a top and skirt for me to try on. A velvety green top and a swirly-coloured skirt.

'A skirt? No, no, *no*. I don't do skirts – only trousers. I'm not getting my legs out for anyone...they're like tree trunks.'

'I'm sure that's not true, Maddy! Anyway, this skirt's quite long – below the knee – so you could try it with these.' She brings out a pair of chunky leather boots with buckles on. 'It'll give the outfit a bit of an edge, contrast with this floaty skirt and no one will see your legs.'

Starr's trying so hard that I don't like to disappoint her. 'OK, I'll try them on just for tonight but I'm warning you – this isn't my style.'

(*Mad's note: Actually I don't even have a style, but if I did, this wouldn't be it.*)

Fifteen minutes later my hair's been pinned up and Starr's giving me a quick makeover. 'Just some eyeliner and a quick slick of lipgloss. *Less is more* – we don't want to overdo it,' she says, expertly dabbing at my face, like a professional stylist.

As soon as I've changed into the clothes she's chosen, she grabs me by the hand and pulls me out into the hall.

'Close your eyes. No peeking until we're in front of the big mirror. I want you to see the full effect.'

I clomp out in my boots, the skirt rustling around my legs making me feel very strange. 'Stand still.' Starr cups her hands over my eyes. 'OK, one, two, three... *Ta daa!*'

'Oh!' I stare in disbelief at an unknown girl who is doing a goldfish impression at me.

'Don't you like it?'

'No...yes I...look so different!' The girl in the mirror is talking. The girl doesn't look beautiful or thin but she looks...interesting. If I saw her in a room I'd think she was worth talking to. Her hair's piled up on her head in a mad, red frizz, but it sort of suits her. And she's wearing a wraparound top which skims her hips and flares out. Her sleeves flare out, too, in a sort of witchy way.

'Oh! I've got curves...' I say in surprise.

'Yes, so make the most of them! Sometimes those huge T-shirts don't do you any favours.'

'And the skirt – it's so swishy but it doesn't look too girly with these boots. I can't believe it. You *are* the High Priestess of Fashion!'

'You shall go to the ball, Cinderella!' Starr says, picking up a hairbrush and waving it around. 'Or, in your case, the charity fashion show. What d'you say Maddy Blue? Are you in?'

I try to push all the feelings of shame, fear and embarrassment to the back of my mind and take a deep breath.

'I'm in,' says the girl in the mirror.

13

RESTYLE YOUR LIFE AND GET CREATIVE

THREE THINGS TO TRY TODAY...

1. Try mixing up some crazy food combos!

The next morning we wake early and I'm craving carbohydrates! We got so carried away with our midnight makeover that we forgot to eat last night – which is a first for me.

At our house breakfast means squashing into our poky little kitchen, plus a mad dash for the cereal box and the last of the milk.

It's different here.

Starr pulls back the curtains and the sun shines in on the large kitchen/diner. Matt and Honey aren't up yet so I sit at the breakfast bar while she fixes breakfast like a celebrity chef. First she juices oranges and grinds coffee beans. Then she lays out strawberries, melon, grapes, banana and kiwi to make an 'exotic fruit breakfast plate'.

'Mmm, it looks lovely and so healthy, but I need chocolate,' I confess.

'No problem, I've got some in this cupboard. Want a piece?'

While she's looking for it I suddenly remember this *Tasty Eats/Foody Treats* feature in one of my mags.

'Have you ever made a sort of fruit kebab and then dipped it in chocolate sauce?' I ask, 'I read about it once but never tried it...'

'Neither have I but it sounds really good!' She hands me the chocolate bar. 'Can you break this up and put it in a cup? We can heat it in a pan of hot water to make the sauce. I'll get some skewers from downstairs.'

Ten minutes later we're dipping our fruit kebabs into the chocolate and they are *yummy*.

Best of all it's just the two of us. No smelly dog, bratty brother or pesky parents to butt in on our *choc-tastic chow-down*. My life is complete!

After we've eaten we sit around chatting and drinking coffee.

'Better make a start on customising those clothes in a minute,' I say when we've lingered as long as we can. 'Scott will be so impressed by our team work.'

Before Starr can answer, the door opens.

'Hi Matt,' Starr says, which is a bit of surprise. I know he must be her dad but he doesn't look like a dad at all.

He looks like someone in a band.

He's got thick, dark, bed-head hair which sticks up at weird angles. His feet are bare and he's wearing frayed jeans and a black T-shirt with faded writing on it. He's tanned like Honey and his eyes are very blue.

'Hey Starr, hey Starr's friend,' he grins sleepily and gives us both a wave. Then he wanders over to a sofa in the main part of the room.

'D'you want some coffee?' Starr asks.

He smiles and nods, then fumbles at the side of the sofa, picks up a guitar and starts strumming softly.

'So how was the salsa night?' Starr asks. Her dad doesn't answer but he starts playing some sad and soulful chords.

She takes the coffee over to him. 'Oh dear, wasn't that bad, was it?'

Again no reply – unless you count the harsh discord he crashes out before throwing the guitar aside.

It says more than words ever can.

Starr looks like someone just switched off her spotlight. I actually see her lose her glow, and her shoulders tense. She holds the coffee cup out to her dad.

'And how did Honey take it?' she asks, trying to sound casual.

Matt takes the coffee and downs it in a few deep gulps. It seems to perk him up a bit because he picks up the guitar again and starts to sing,

**'When nothing is right and things don't go your way –
you gotta wait for the sunshine at the break of day.
Yeah, wake for the sunshine at the break of day –
when nothing and no one is going your way.'**

Then he carries on strumming, sitting in the sun, lost in the music.

I remember Starr describing how Matt and Honey met when he was busking round Spain. It's easy to see why Honey fell for him.

Listening to him sing makes everything seem all right. Starr puts the dishes in the sink and starts to wash up so I grab a tea towel to help. She's taken her cue from the music and seems determined to carry on as normal.

'Shall we sort through those clothes and pick out the ones we want to customise?' she says when we're done. 'We can do it in my room. I'll get the stuff.'

♥ ★ ♡

We've just about sorted everything when the shouting begins.

Honey must be up now because I can hear her voice sounding sharp and angry. I can't hear what they're saying through the walls but Matt replies now and again in a low rumble.

Starr stops what she's doing and slumps down on a chair. She closes her eyes tight like she's shutting out the world.

I wait a bit and then sit next to her. 'You OK?'

She sighs, 'I'm sick of all this arguing, that's all. Honey's so stressed about everything at the moment.'

RE-STYLE YOUR LIFE AND GET CREATIVE!

2. Try changing your plans.

Do something on the spur of the moment – the results might surprise you!

I wonder if I should invite her round to my place for a bit, but I'm not sure. Scott's the only friend who's ever had the pleasure of entering the *Maddy Blue Madhouse*.

I hesitate for a moment but then I can hear Lifecoach Laura's voice in my head reminding me that Starr's my friend now, too.

'Um...would it help if we worked at my house today? There's not much room and I've got a bratty brother and a smelly dog but—'

'It's down to *you*, Matt.' Honey must be out in the hall now because her voice is even louder and I can't compete. '*You* lost the money. *You* came running home to Mummy and Daddy. We could have made something of our lives and now we're stuck in this bloody backwater—'

We hear a door slam and next thing Honey walks into

the room. She's still in her dressing gown and without her make-up I can see the strain showing on her face.

She narrows her eyes. 'Did Matt tell you about our *sensational* salsa night, then, Starr?'

'Not exactly.'

'No. Well we only had two couples turn up. Two couples – after all that publicity! So I decided to have the demo-dance down in the main bar to show the customers what we can do. Halfway through it some drunken yobs decided it would be really hilarious to gate-crash the bar and join in.'

She looks at me as if it's my fault, adding, 'Welcome to Westfield.'

'Next time might be different,' Starr says.

'Next time? On no, you haven't heard the end of the story. When we tried to chuck them out they turned nasty. Throwing bottles and scaring the customers. We ended up calling the police! I was clearing up the damage till half past one this morning... So, no more Salsa evenings,' she shrugs and all the fight seems to go out of her.

Then she looks round at the piles of clothes in Starr's room and the pictures of magazine models on the walls. There's a picture of Honey, too, looking young and carefree on a beach somewhere. I was so impressed last night when Starr told me it was her mum.

'Don't make the mistakes I have, Starr. If modelling's a way out for you, don't waste it...'

When Honey closes the door we don't say a word.

I look at Starr but her face is closed-up, like she doesn't want to talk. She starts to put the clothes in bags.

'Maddy, you know you said we could work round at your place today?' Her voice is casual and she's too busy to look at me.

'Yes?'

'Well, I think that's a good idea...if the offer still stands?'

'Grrrrrr!'

Max growls at Starr when I open my front door.

'Sorry, he thinks he's a dog,' I mutter through gritted teeth, trying to smile as if it's perfectly normal.

Now I'm wondering if it was such a good idea to invite Starr round. I don't want my loony brother to upset her when she's feeling so fragile. He's someone who takes some getting used to.

'You're very fierce – are you a guard dog?' she asks, playing along.

He pulls a face, 'Not a dog, I'm a dinosaur.'

(Mad's Note: Typical - crazy and contrary, too!)

'Lucky I bought some dinosaur food, then,' Starr says reaching into her bag and pulling out a mandarin orange.

Max watches as she peels it and offers him a piece.

He grabs it, pops it into his mouth and then skitters into the kitchen, suddenly shy.

That was very impressive. I think Max likes her – well he's stopped guarding the door, anyway. I lead her over the doorstep and into the hall, but it's as if I'm seeing it through Starr's eyes now and I realise it's a total tip. Max's toys are everywhere and there are coats and shoes all over the hall. It all looks so dark and dingy after Starr's bright and airy flat.

Mum comes bustling out from the kitchen, followed by a smelly dog and a growling brother. Mum must have been cooking because she's tied her hair back in that flowery scarf I hate. It's not exactly the height of fashion and her hair! – it's frizzled grey which makes her look older than she is and she's not exactly a young mum like Honey, anyway. I've told her to get a colour-rinse but she says she'd rather *'grow old gracefully'*.

'Starr, thank you so much for having Maddy to stay last night!' she says, like I'm five years old. 'As soon as she phoned to say you were coming over but you don't eat meat, I told her not to worry. I found a lovely veggie recipe I've been meaning to try for ages, so we'll make sure you don't starve... We picked some herbs from the garden, didn't we Maxi?'

'Grrrarrr!'

'Oops, I forgot, it's Max-asauraus now isn't it?'

Max doesn't answer, he's eating the rest of the mandarin orange and Starr's stroking Chester.

'Then we just needed a handful of rice and—'

Yawn-arama!

Why does she always do that? Not only does Mum force-feed every visitor to the house but she always has to talk them through the recipe, too.

Now Dad's coming out into the hallway and he's yet another representative of the *Old Fogey's Fashion House* in his knitted waistcoat and baggy cord trousers. He shakes Starr's hand and introduces himself as Gerald Blue, like he's at a royal garden party or something.

'Ah, so you're the girl who lives in *Bar Salsa*. Now, there's an interesting history to that place. It's built on the site of the old Westfield town prison. It's marked on one of the maps in my office.'

Double Yawn-arama!

Now he's telling her that he works for the Museums Department! How's that compare to a model and a musician? Mum and Dad look like an old pair of relics themselves, compared to Matt and Honey.

Please can I turn back time, like you can turn back the page of a magazine? Then I'd never make the mistake of inviting Starr to my house!

'So what was it you said you were doing after lunch?' Mum's saying.

'Customising our clothes,' I mutter.

'The ones we got in charity shops,' Starr adds.

'Oh yes, I approve of recycling.'

'It's more than that, Mum. We're totally *restyling* them to make them unique. Tie-dying and fabric painting and ripping and sewing and adding some sparkle – that's customising!'

Max suddenly starts leaping around like a loon when he hears this, shouting, 'Sparkl-ising! I want to sparklise too!'

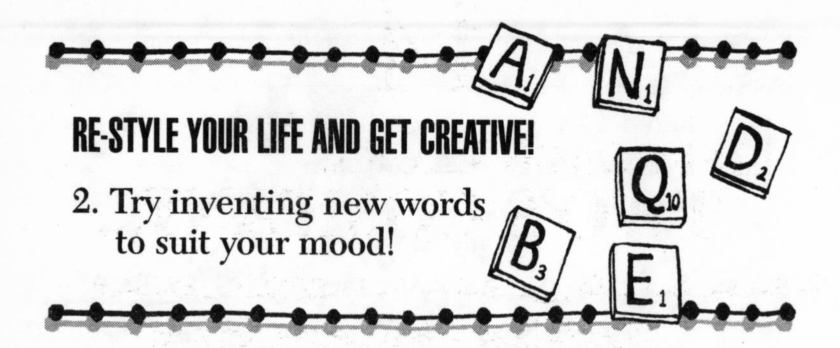

RE-STYLE YOUR LIFE AND GET CREATIVE!

2. Try inventing new words to suit your mood!

Mum and Dad start beaming and chuckling at their darling dinosaur and his made-up words. Yuk – it's all so cringey-cutsie that I want to throw up.

I think of Starr – OK, her parents fight sometimes, but whose don't? I still think they're both completely cool. Unlike my lot. What's she going to think of me now?

I risk a look over at her and – **surprise-a-mundo** – she's laughing too.

In fact she's not just laughing.

She looks happy and she's got her glow back.

Yes, I've got to say it...

She's sparklising!

14

LIFECOACH LAURA: TWO'S COMPANY...

Lifecoach Laura – Two's company...but three doesn't have to be a crowd.

How to manage a three-way friendship.

'Communication is important,' says Lifecoach Laura. 'Tell each other everything and don't hold back...'

'So how was it?' Scott asks when we're back to reality and walking to school together on Monday morning.

'It was...*magical*,' I say and wait for his reaction.

His eyebrows shoot up. 'Come again?'

'Well, you were right and I was wrong. Starr's not like I thought she was. *There's more to that girl than meets the eye*, as my mum said yesterday. And she must have worked some kind of spell on me because I've agreed to be a model in the show, after all.'

'Praise the Lord,' Scott says in mock-preacher mode. *'It's a miracle!'*... But how come your mum said that about Starr? I thought you were round at *Bar Salsa* this weekend.'

'Yeah, we were – we had a proper girly night in, trying on clothes and stuff. Oh, and I met her parents – not that they look old enough to be parents – they're so cool. But in the morning everything changed and we just had to get out.'

'Why? What happened?'

'Honestly Scott. When I woke up it was like I'd walked into a TV soap! Starr's dad was just sitting at the kitchen table, strumming a guitar and looking lost. Honey was completely the opposite – all strung-out and stressy. She looked terrible, like she'd slept in her make-up.

'What was wrong? D'you know?'

'Apparently the Red Hot Salsa night was a disaster. Hardly anyone turned up except a few drunks who tried to trash the place. Honey went mental – said she hated it here and it was all his fault – I thought she was going to throw something!'

'How did Starr take it? Was she OK?'

'*Mmm,* she seemed to be. Said she was used to it and Honey would calm down in a day or two. We were going to call you but we thought you'd be busy with the set. So we went over to mine – which was just as mental but in a different way.'

'Hmm, so is Max still having those I-am-a-dog days?'

'Oh no, he's grown out of that.'

'Well that's something—'

'Now he's a dinosaur.'

'Oh.'

'Yeah, but Starr thought that was sweet. In fact,

she thought everything was wonderful. The way my mum kept trying to force-feed us all day, my dad's lectures on the *History of Westfield,* the dog, our tiny cramped kitchen...'

'So, what did you get up to at your place?'

'Ooh we were being dead creative – tie-dyeing T-shirts, ripping off sleeves and drawing on bags and shoes with fabric pens.'

'It's good to spend time apart from friends but try not to make them feel left out,' says Lifecoach Laura. *'A little present or a kind thought will reassure them.'*

'And we made this for you to wear at the show...'

Scott opens the bag I give him and holds up a white T-shirt. He reads what it says on the front.

'Set the World on Fire! Westfield School Fashion Show'

'We did the letters and this design here,' I say, pointing to some flickering red and yellow flames.

'Hey, I'm touched. Thank you.'

'I came up with the slogan to give the show a theme. Starr wanted it to look really good, to prove to her mum she's more than just a pretty face.'

'How d'you mean?'

'Starr wants to be a fashion designer and it's like this is her first collection. We even made a mood board yesterday—'

'Which is...?'

'Oh, something to stick on scraps of fabric and pictures from mags to inspire us. We're using a seasonal theme with a twist. Think fireworks and divali lights, as well as autumn leaves. We don't want people to hear the word 'charity' and think boring. We want to give it some excitement and sparkle!'

'You're really enjoying all this, aren't you, Maddy?'

'Mmm, Starr's made me see fashion in a different way. I'm not trying to impress any more, I'm going to dress to express.'

'Express what?'

'Ooh, I don't know. The secret inner me! I sewed some tiny mirrors and sequins on my skirt and top. That's like all the hidden fires you have inside you – the bit that sparklises.'

I stop. Scott's giving me a funny look. 'Oh, just tell me to shut up. You wouldn't get it unless you were there. Sorry, we got a bit silly yesterday – it must be a girl thing.'

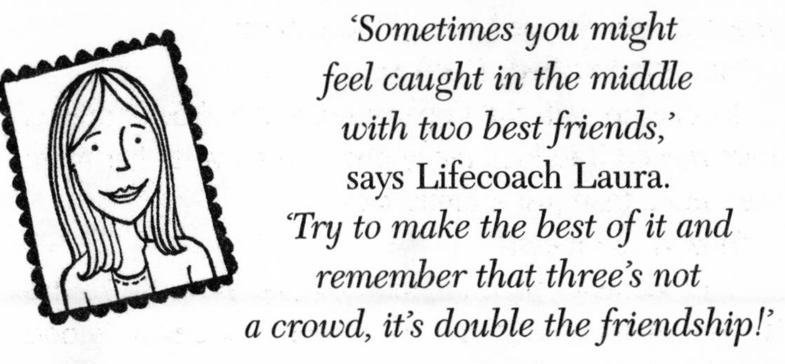

Scott shakes his head. 'No, it's OK. That's deep, y'know. Respect. I think you and Starr are going to be real friends. I'm happy for you.'

And for a second there Scott looks sad but then he smiles and I can't be sure of what I saw.

We're nearly at school now and Starr's waiting at the gates and waving.

'Thanks,' I whisper. 'But we go back a long way, Scott, and don't you forget it. Best friends forever, OK?'

'Ok,' he says and punches me on the shoulder.

It hurts a bit, so I know he really means it.

(Mad's note: Are you sure about that...)

15

TRUE CONFESSIONS – THE WORST DAY OF MY LIFE!

Tear-jerking true life stories

Get your tissues ready...

I'm not sure of anything any more.

I'm sitting at home on my bed in a total trauma. I can't believe what happened today. It was just like one of those shock-horror, slice of life stories in a teen magazine. The type you think they must have made up, because things like that don't happen in real life, do they?

Well, now I know that they do...

I keep going over and over the last few weeks in my head looking for clues but I can't find anything. Things were going so well – Starr and I met up after school almost every night to work on the clothes for the show. We used her hall-of-mirrors space, too, for dancing.

Yes, Maddy Blue salsa dancing – who would have believed it after my first lumpy-bump bonanza?

But Starr said it would help me get into shape and move better on the catwalk and she was right. All the models in the show practised together and I can wiggle my hips with the best of them now.

Actually my hips aren't quite as big as they once were either. All that dancing and less time lazing has left me – well not exactly model-girl slim – but...curvy. Fat but fit, if you know what I mean.

So things were going well with Starr and even though we didn't see much of Scott he was busy too, wasn't he?

So, how did...?

I don't want to think about it.

I don't want to write about it, either.

Or if I do I want to edit it so I can pretend it happened to someone else...

Someone who doesn't give her real name...

The Worst Day of My Life

This month M.B.*, from Westfield, re-lives the day her life went from good, to bad, to...off-the-scale nightmare!

(*Name withheld)

It was all going so well. I was working on a fashion show to raise money for a children's ward in a local hospital. As the show grew nearer I started to feel like I was really fitting in – with my clothes and with other people, too.

And I had TWO best friends now – Scott and Starr. Working together on the show made us all so close…

How could I know it would tear our friendship apart?

One big happy family?

It happened at our final dress rehearsal when we tried out all the clothes, music and lighting. Some people from our year were coming to watch – and some teachers, too – so we wanted to get it right.

Where's Starr?

There was a real buzz as we got changed after school. We turned the music up extra loud to get in the mood and I was fizzing with nerves and excitement.

Usually Starr helped me pin my hair up but she wasn't around. I guessed she was with Scott, sorting out some last-minute changes somewhere, so I went off to find them. Scott was doing the lights for the show but he wasn't around backstage and neither was Starr yet. Up in the lighting box I could see two shadows so I climbed the steps to see if they were there. Halfway up I saw the two shadows merge into one… I couldn't believe what I was seeing!

All loved-up

I carried on climbing – hoping against hope that I'd made a mistake – but no… As I got nearer I could see Scott had his arm round Starr – he was stroking her hair and whispering as she snuggled into his chest.

I CAUGHT MY BEST FRIENDS IN A CLINCH!!!!

I turned round and clattered down the stairs. Scott called out my name but whatever he had to say, I didn't want to hear. It was too much to take in and I needed time to get used to the idea.

My two best friends were all loved-up!

I knew I should be happy for them, but I wasn't. All I could think was that it left me right out in the cold.

Three minus two = one left over.

Jealousy junkie

I ran to the changing rooms and clawed off my customised clothes like they were on fire. My brain kicked in with lots of questions and suddenly I got really angry. How long had this been going on? Why didn't they tell me? Weren't we supposed to be best friends?

Yes, I admit it – I was a jealousy junkie!

At that moment I decided there was only one way to stop my addiction – cut myself off from anything to do with them.

I looked round desperately for a change of clothes and pulled on my old jeans. They were getting too big for me now – so they could be auctioned off, no problem.

New image

Now, I needed a top to wear and that's when my true best friend came to the rescue. I pulled out my latest

mag from my bag, tore off the wrapper and scanned the words,

ZAP

Dazzle like a firework in our red hot boob tube! Free matching lippy too.

Perfectamundo!

Then I dashed for a private cubicle, holding my mag in front of me.

Normally I'd never wear something as revealing as a boob tube in my life but nothing was normal now.

The top was a skin-tight fit – even when I took off my bra I had to struggle into it. That should have set alarm bells ringing but time was running out – someone was banging on the door so I didn't have time to think.

Daring and glamorous

'M. you're on in one minute!'

'Coming!' I yelled, yanking my hair up into a ponytail and smudging the lippy on.

In my new red top and lip gloss I felt daring and glamorous. Dazzling like a firework, like the mag said. There was no time for a reality check in the mirror, the music was starting up, so I ran to the wings in my bare feet.

Starr was there looking pale and upset (maybe she felt guilty after I caught her out?) and she was obviously surprised by my quick change.

'M. what are you wearing? Why—?'

I blanked Starr completely. 'Tania, can I borrow your sandals, pleeaase? You can have them back as soon as I've finished.'

Tania slipped them off and kicked them over.

'M. don't go on like that—'

'Sorry Starr, that's my cue,' I squeezed my feet into the high strappy sandals and stood up straight. 'Gotta go!'

Magazine dream

It was weird. I didn't feel a bit nervous, even though some teachers were sitting in the front row, along with half my class. I was on a jealousy-fuelled adrenalin-rush and nothing could stop me.

I'd stepped into girl-world and was living the magazine dream!

Meet M. the model – she looks perfect and can't put a foot wrong!

I swaggered on stage salsa-swaying to the music and the crowd started clapping.

This is it! They love me!

I sashayed to the front of the stage and hip-wiggled for eight beats before my big turn. I knew Scott was watching from up there in the lighting box and Starr was in the wings. This was to prove that I didn't need them any more…

Catwalk catastrophe

Then I did a sort of defiant twirl and the crowd went wild! The noise must have gone to my head because I flung out my foot in a high kick and – Oops! Nightmare Scenario! – my sandal shot out right into the crowd and hit the Head – Smack! – on the head!

Cringerama!!

At the same I lost my balance and tripped backwards – Rripp! – and my boob-tube exploded, tearing open at the seams!

Double blusherama!!!

Now my model girl dream was in tatters. Just like the bits of boob-tube I was clutching in front of me to cover my embarrassment!

Major booberama!!!!

Somehow I staggered to my feet and hobbled off stage – the sound of cheering and whistling in my ears.

Diva-drama loserama!!!!!

THIS IS A TRUE STORY – IT HAPPENED TO ME! THE WORST DAY OF MY LIFE…AND MY MOST EMBARRASSING MOMENT ALL ROLLED INTO ONE!!!

(Mad's note: If this story has raised any issues for you, please phone our helpline for the next available plane, train or boat out of the country.)

16

BARE-FACED CHIC

Stressed? Depressed? Is your life a mess?

... Time to feng-shui your life and start afresh! Take a good look around you and clean up.

First, decide what stays
and what's to throw away...

Thinking about it now I don't know whether to laugh or cry. Well, I'm all cried out now, anyway. Just a few dry, hiccuppy sobs left.

It's so typical of me, though. I can't even manage a true-life tragedy without turning it into a cartoon comedy.

So here I am. Still hunched on my bed with a coat over my bare shoulders. Arms crossed, legs crossed, a stupid strappy sandal dangling from one foot.

How did I get here? Where did the coat come from?

Dunno...next question. When I got backstage after the catwalk catastrophe everything flashed by really fast – like the pictures in a magazine when you flick through the pages.

People. Faces. Words. A meaningless blur.

I just ran (or hopped...the other sandal's probably been arrested by now). And here I am.

I look at the mirror and see the face of a clown. My hair's all scraped back to reveal a round, white dinner-plate face. My make-up's a mess – tear-smeared black panda-eyes and a scarlet lippy-smudged mouth.

I turn away only to find hundreds of clear-eyed, clear-skinned cover-girls grinning up at me from the stacks of magazines all over the floor.

Snappy, zappy phrases are shouting in my face,

Hot new hairstyles!

Perfect party fashion!

Brilliant beauty buys!

Ten tips for lush lips!

Go for glam!

Flirty new looks!

Why can't they just shut up?

Suddenly I'm angry.

Lies.

Everyone is lying to me –

Scott

Starr

Lifecoach Laura and these stupid magazines with all their fake dreams.

I pick up a mag and tear it straight down the spine.

Rrrrip!
Then another and another.

Rrrrip! Rrrrip!
Pages scatter everywhere –

Fashion, **PASSION**, **Problems**, Cringes, **Confessions**, *Obsessions*, **CELEBRITIES**, Stars, **Gossip** and **FREE GIFTS**...

When all the pages are torn to pieces I feel calmer. In the bathroom I scrub my face bare and yank the sparkly band out of my hair. Then I change my clothes and go downstairs to get a black plastic sack.

Clear out the clutter in your room
Don't delay – do it today!

BAG IT, BIN IT AND
MAKE SPACE FOR CHANGE

Down in the kitchen Max starts pestering. 'What doing?'

'Nothing.'

'Why you got that bag?'

'Oh just chucking out some stuff.'

'Why?'

'Because.'

'Why?'

By now Max is trotting upstairs after me. This conversation could go on for ever so I decide to end it now.

'Max, don't come in my room. Go back to your kennel or jungle or whatever.' (I can't tell if he's a dog or a dinosaur today.)

Max stands at the door on tiptoe and looks in. The floor is a colourful carpet of shredded mags.

'*Oooh*, what doing?'

'*Nothing!*' I start picking up pieces and stuffing them into my bag.

'Sparklising!' Max says, getting the wrong idea. 'Max help too!'

He bounces in all excited, slipping and sliding on the glossy paper.

'Calm down, will you?' I say as he gets more and more excited.

'Sparklising! Sparklising!'

He's completely carried away with himself now and slithering around dangerously.

I stand up. 'Max, be careful, you'll—'

Too late. He lands off balance and his legs slide away beneath him.

'Whump!'

His head bangs on the back of my cupboard and he slams to the floor. As I rush over I see his eyeballs disappear into the back of his head and his eyelids flicker shut.

That's when the screaming starts.

But it's not Max.

It's me.

Please let him be OK. Please let him be OK. Please let him be OK. Please—

I'm sitting in casualty when my phone rings and shocks me back to the moment.

It's Scott.

'Maddy, how's Max – is he all right?'

'I don't know. He was knocked out cold but he came round a bit on the drive over. Mum and Dad are in with him now – he's having an x-ray, but how did you know...?'

'My mum – a.k.a. Nurse Hyacinth Lord? She asked your parents if I could give you a call. Said you might need a friend.'

'Yes...yes p...please,' that's all I can manage. I read in some mag that we're seventy per cent water but I'm about one hundred per cent just now.

'I'm on my way,' he says and hangs up.

Get clutter-free and see things differently

Take some time to work out what really matters to you!

Some time later I look up to see Nurse Hyacinth Lord bringing her son into the children's ward. He's as tall as her now and I wonder when that happened.

'Here you are, young lady. Tell him all your worries – he's a very good listener.'

'Mum!' Scott looks embarrassed and also confused.

'So where's Max? And your Mum and Dad?'

Hyacinth starts chuckling and even I manage a smile.

Now Scott looks at us in astonishment.

'What's going on?'

'Children, they always bounce back! Just like you, Scott, when you were a *lickle bwoy,*' Hyacinth teases, squeezing his cheek.

'Mum, give it a rest!' Scott pleads.

She holds up her hands, 'Can't stand here talking all day, some of us got work to do. You can tell him the good news, Maddy, that's all I'm saying.'

I wave at her as she disappears down the corridor. 'Your mum's been great. It was so good to see a friendly face when we got here—'

'So is he all right, then?' Scott interrupts. 'Where is he?'

We can't keep him in suspense any longer, so I take him over to the window of the children's playroom.

'Look in there!' I say pointing, 'You won't believe it.'

Inside Max is standing up, happily piling bricks on to a tower he's building with Mum and Dad.

'I can't believe it myself,' I say. 'One minute he's all limp and lifeless, the next minute he comes out of x-ray, sits up and asks if he can go and play!'

'So were the x-rays clear?'

'Yes, no damage – just a bump on the head the size of a dinosaur's egg. They want him to stay in for a few hours' observation but he's fine now. In fact he's hyper, so the playroom's a lifesaver!'

'Yes and it'll be even better after our fashion show.'

'Mmm, the toys have obviously been lovingly used by thousands of kids... Your mum was telling me how much they're looking forward to buying some new ones.'

'Depends on what money we raise in...' Scott looks at his watch, 'oh, less than twenty-four hours. No pressure.'

Suddenly the memory of a strappy sandal flying through the air smacks me full-on and I gasp. Max's accident made me forget all about my own one at the show.

'Oh no, the Head! – is he all right, is he dead?'

'Yeah, laughed his head off.'

'What?'

'It's all cool Maddy, luckily he saw the funny side of things – but what is it with you and head injuries today?'

'I don't know! I blame myself for Max – he slipped over in my room – but Mum said they're going to fix a lock on my door so he knows when to keep out. And

I hate to think about the dress rehearsal... Maddy-Mess-Up, prancing about on stage like a baby elephant!'

'Actually you went down really well – if you'll pardon the pun.'

Max spots us from the playroom and waves. I wave back.

'Maddy, can I have a word with you before we go in,' Scott whispers. 'It's about earlier when you saw me with—'

'Better not disappoint the little livewire,' I say, pushing the playroom door open before he can finish. I'm so glad Scott is here tonight but I don't think I could cope with an update on his love life on top of everything else.

Max comes running over and a bouncy bundle of boy is in my arms and I'm hugging him tight.

'Hug Scott too!' Max says.

I move closer to Scott who puts his arms round us both, saying, 'I thought you'd never ask!'

(Mad's note: Cheesy hug-fest with extra cheese topping, or what?)

After that Max proudly shows us his bump and asks us to push him around in a toy car with one wheel missing...

It's hard work and it takes two of us but luckily the doctor appears before long. She checks Max over and gives him the all-clear, so it's time to go. Dad offers Scott a lift home but it turns out that Hyacinth clocked off her shift half an hour ago, so he can go home with her. There's no time for us to have the heart-to-heart Scott wanted after all, and I must admit it's a relief.

'Do you think you'll make it to school in the morning?' Scott asks, as we all say our goodbyes in the car park. 'It's been a long day today and tomorrow won't exactly be easy.'

He's right, I'm dreading showing my face at school tomorrow! First there's my famous *flip-trip-rip-and-strip* routine at the show – and second I've got to get used to seeing Scott and Starr together as a couple. I wonder why she's not here tonight but guess that Scott didn't tell her what happened. Maybe he was being tactful, who knows?

Anyway, for once I'm not thinking about me. What's important is raising money for toys on the children's ward and not letting my friends down.

'Of course I'll be there – the show must go on!' I grin.

'Good on you, girl,' Scott says. 'See you in the morning – we've got unfinished business to discuss.'

17

GETTING READY FOR A BIG NIGHT OUT?

We get home around ten and the first thing I do is finish clearing up my room. When I've finally got rid of every scrap of paper, at last I can see the colour of my carpet and my room is totally mag-free.

Or is it?

Two seconds after climbing into bed I sit up straight and switch on the light. I've suddenly remembered that my newest mag – the one with the free exploding boob-tube – is in my bag.

How can I sleep while it's still in my room?

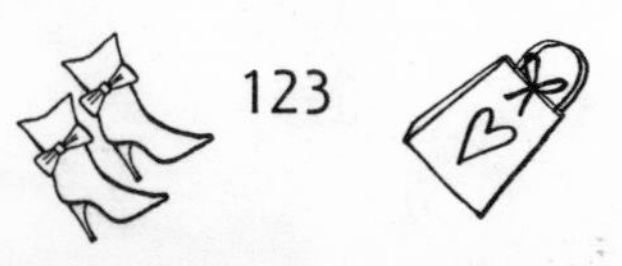

I fish around at the side of the bed, pull it out and start flicking through it with new eyes.

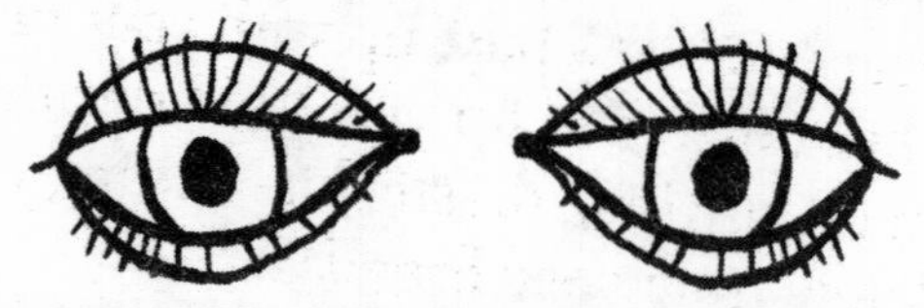

Why was I such a mag-hag?

What did I ever see in them? Trashy fashions, model-girl-clones and unbelievable problem pages – it's going to be such a joy to rip it to pieces...

And then something jumps out at me,

A letter written by the starry-eyed mag-hag I once was. The one I wrote when I thought Scott blabbed my secret dream to be a catwalk queen. I scan down to the end and there's my name – M. B. (Miserable and Blue).

I know the answer is out of date but I read it anyway.

Dear Miserable and Blue.

Sorry to hear you had a bust-up with your mates. It happens, but don't give up yet. Find out the facts before you do anything drastic like cutting yourself off completely from your friends.

You say you knew things would go wrong, ever since this new girl joined your gang. Perhaps this is bothering you more than you think?

Are you're turning into a jealousy junkie? Remember that a healthy friendship has room for other people too – or you risk becoming stale mates.

Good Luck
Lifecoach Laura x

When I've finished reading I fold it carefully and put it at the side of my bed. It's the first thing I'll see when I wake up and I want to read it through again.

It's not out of date.

Lifecoach Laura's right.

I *am* a jealousy junkie but tomorrow I'm kicking the habit. It's going to be hard seeing Scott and Starr together but I don't want to lose their friendship so I'll just have to put on a brave face.

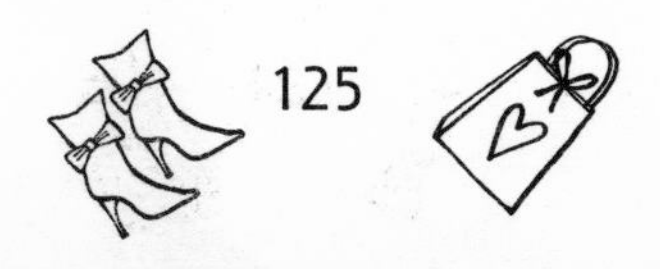

True to his word, Scott knocks on my door right on time next morning. I practise my smile and wait for him to raise the unspoken subject that lies between us. It doesn't take long,

'Maddy, before we get to school I just want to talk to you about yesterday. When you saw me with Starr, it wasn't—'

'It's all right, Scott, you don't have to explain. You and Starr are an item now. I know it and I accept it. You don't have to worry that I'll turn into the *screaming green mag-hag from hell*. I've got used to the idea and—'

'Maddy, you're wrong, we're not an item. I don't think of Starr in that way!'

'Why not? She's pretty and slim and talented – if I didn't fancy boys, I'd fancy her! What's wrong with you?'

'Nothing – thank you very much! But I'm not going to get distracted from my work just yet. I'm aiming high and—'

'But I *saw* you together. You can't deny that. You were kissing and cuddling and canoodling and—'

'It was a hug! A comforting hug, that's what friends do remember? Especially when one of them's had bad news.'

'What bad news? What are you talking about?'

'I'd rather Starr told you herself. If we walk quickly you can have a word with her – she's waiting for you.'

'Where?'

'I reckon this is a girl-thing. She's chosen somewhere that's off-limits for me.'

We get to school in record time and Starr's hanging around inside the girls' toilets.

She's lost her glow again and I'm beginning to suspect what's happened already.

'Not the best place for a heart-to-heart is it?' I say. Even as I speak someone pushes between us and starts washing their hands at the sink.

We move out into the corridor but it's not much better here either. 'Shall we try the library?'

She nods and we find two comfy chairs behind some book shelves where no one will disturb us.

'Sorry about Max,' she says. 'I would have come to the hospital only—'

'What's happened?' I ask. I can see she's close to tears.

'Honey's gone.'

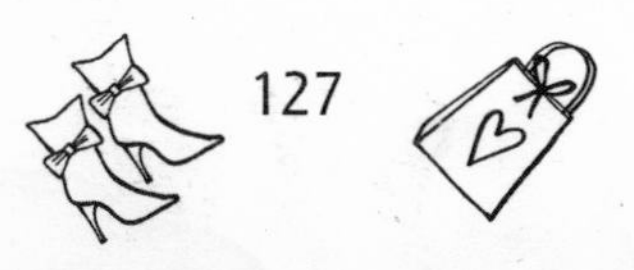

'Oh,' I had suspected it might be trouble at home. 'What d'you mean? Where—?'

Starr takes a deep breath and starts again. 'They had an argument and Honey walked out. She's staying with her sister in London. She phoned me out of the blue yesterday. I was with Scott when she called...' Her eyes fill up and she can't say any more.

'Oh Starr, I'm so sorry,' and now I'm hugging her and I know what Scott means.

A comforting hug. It's what friends do.

'So...has she done this sort of thing before?' I ask when she seems to have recovered a little.

'No, they've argued quite a lot recently but she's never walked out. That's what I'm worried about. I think it's serious this time. She asked me to go down and see her at the weekend...'

'Are you going?' I say trying to keep calm but inside I'm building up to a *manic-panic*.

What if Honey says she's leaving Matt? What if Starr never comes back?

'I don't know... I told her we'd got the show tonight but she said she was sorry, she just couldn't face it. Dad can't get away from the bar either...'

What a mess. I want to start crying with Starr but now is not the time for a soggy-sobbing session. I'm her friend and it's up to me to help her.

I think of all the pages of advice I've read from Lifecoach Laura and I think of all the fashion shoots in all my magazines...

'We could film it,' I say. 'Then you can send a copy to Honey and show it to your dad! Wait till they see all your *Glam-tastic* clothes, they'll be so proud of you they'll...'

I don't finish the sentence. Somehow I hope that it'll bring them to their senses. Make them think – *how can we split-up when we've created such a talented daughter?* But even I'm not stupid enough to believe it's really that simple.

'Yes, I think Honey would really like that.' Starr's dabbing at her eyes with a tissue and I can tell she's really going for the idea. 'I can take it down with me to London and Matt can have a copy too. But how can we sort it? The show's tonight and—'

Now my mind's fizzing with ideas like one of those *A Thousand Things to do in the Holidays!* pages in one of my mags.

'Leave it to me. I can sell it to the Head as a money-making idea for the show. And funnily enough I've been told he wants to see me after registration this morning. It'll help me with my major-grovelling...'

The meeting with the Head isn't as bad as I expect. I tell him how sorry I am and offer him a *super spot cover-stick* to hide his bruise which he seems to appreciate.

(Mad's note: It's a free-gift I blagged from the librarian who'd just had a new delivery of magazines that morning.)

Then I tell him about my idea to film the show and sell copies to make more money for the hospital. I even

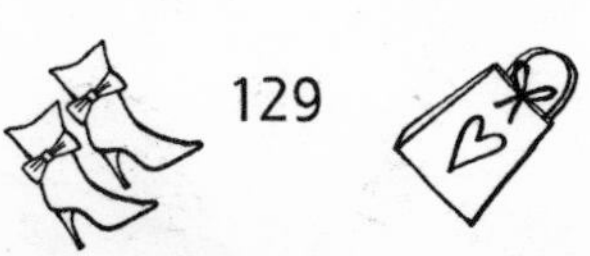

describe Max driving round in the broken car so he can see we need every penny we can get!

He really likes the idea and says we can borrow school equipment. Then I get even more carried away and offer to do the filming too. When he asks about my modelling part in the show I realise it doesn't matter to me any more.

'I just don't think I'm cut out to be model material,' I confess. 'But I have a friend who'd be perfect to take my place…'

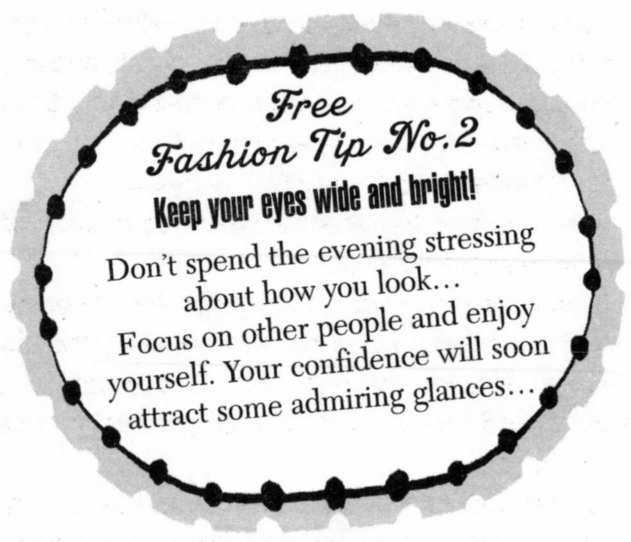

The hall's filling up with parents, teachers and pupils and I'm concentrating hard on holding the camera and catching everything.

Out in the audience Max turns round and sticks his tongue out. Mum waves and Dad gives me a wink as they settle down in the front row. I wave back at them and

I don't care if anyone sees – even if they are the most embarrassing family in the world.

Things look different now and I want this to be the best fashion show ever. Not just for Scott but for Starr, too, and her mum and dad.

♥ ★ ♡

Music's pumping out at full volume but when Scott hits the multicoloured spotlight it suddenly goes quiet.

I focus in on the Head's head as he walks on stage and introduces the show. You can hardly see his bruise at all so the *super spot-cover stick* must have worked a treat.

'Good evening, everyone and welcome to Autumn Fires – The Westfield Charity Fashion Show.'

Everyone claps like mad and Max barks but I don't think anyone hears except me.

'A great deal of hard work, energy and creativity has gone into staging this show and restyling the clothes you'll see tonight,' he says. 'I've already seen a dress rehearsal and I must say it knocked me out,' he touches his forehead.

Bag over face time!! Instant blush!! Everyone's laughing but then someone in my class gives me a nod and whispers, 'You'll have to try harder next time, Maddy!'

Even I have to smile and my face cools by a few degrees. At least the Head's alive and can make a joke of it.

'Clothes will be auctioned during the show,' the Head continues. 'Write down your bids and our helpers will

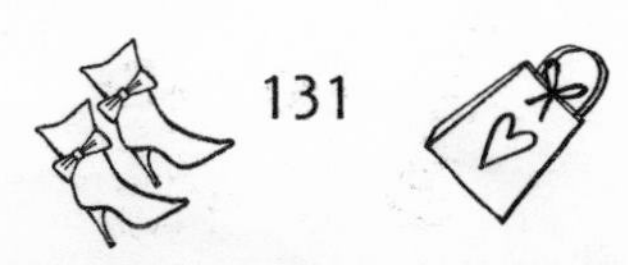

come round to collect them. Please give generously. All proceeds will go towards new toys and games for Westfield Hospital Children's Ward.'

I sweep round and focus on Scott's mum. Her face is beaming with pride and I'm glad I caught the moment.

Then the salsa music starts pounding as I track back to the stage and catch the models lining up and posing like professionals.

The spotlights pick out Starr's key colours – hot reds, deep purples, bold greens, dark blues and flickers of silver and gold. Everyone looks so grown-up and good-looking when they're not in school uniform. Paris, New York, Milan – eat your heart out!

The show flashes by like the fashion pages in a glossy magazine.

ADD SPARKLE TO YOUR WARDROBE!

DAZZLING DETAIL!

Fashion to tie-dye for!

Cool ways to customise your clothes!

Rip, slash and splash on colour!

DIY Divas

Then a familiar salsa track starts up and I recognise my cue.

Just hearing that music makes my hands shake as memories of my *catwalk catastrophe* flood back. But I take

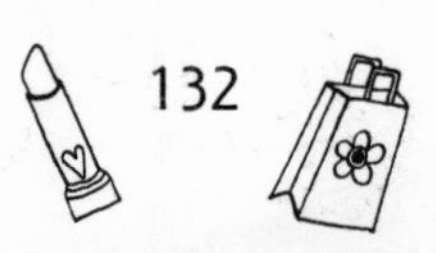

a deep breath and breathe slowly. I've got to get a grip and hold steady. It's important not to mess up this time. I promised my friends I'd get it right...

When Starr walks on stage she's found her glow. Her face is lit-up and I know she's trying extra-hard for Honey and Matt. I can see from my digital screen that the camera loves her. She's moving and swaying like a supermodel and smiling like a true star. Only Scott and I would ever know how upset she is about what happened at home.

Honey's right – Starr's got something. It's a shame she and Matt aren't here to see their own daughter in action but at least this is the next best thing. I'm glad she agreed to take my part.

Finally the stage empties and the Head reappears so I focus in on him again.

'Thank you all for coming tonight. The students did us proud and we've made twice as much money this year for our chosen charity.'

I pan round as everyone claps and cheers.

'And special thanks to the students who really made this happen. Firstly Scott Lord for the organisation and lighting.'

I track Scott coming on stage. He looks relieved and happy now it's all over. I'm so proud of him. Ever since I've known him he's always managed to ignore all the

distractions in life and keep focussed on what matters. Like now – raising money for a really worthwhile cause.

When the cheering calms down, the Head speaks again. 'Secondly Starr Child for costume design and choreography.'

Now I'm tracking Starr as she shakes hands with the Head and gives Scott a hug.

(Mad's note: I'm OK with that... I'm kicking the jealousy habit, honest.)

In fact I'm proud of Starr, too. She's so talented and artistic but she doesn't show off about it. Between the two of them I've got such brilliant friends – Scott's got the common-sense and Starr adds the sparkle. I wonder what on earth they must see in me?

'Finally I'd like Maddy Blue to come on stage,' the Head continues. 'Starr and Scott told me earlier that the fashion show came from her suggestion which was a real flash of inspiration! Not only that, she asked if we could film it too and many of you want copies, which will make the final sum collected even higher. So, let's hear a big thank you for Maddy and all her bright ideas!'

It's not easy to hold the camera steady when people are patting you on the back and cheering in your face but I'm a professional and hang on in there. It's still in my hand when I'm swept up on stage, but Scott takes it off me so I can shake hands with the Head.

Everyone's cheering and here I am up on stage in my old clothes which aren't so flattering on my lady lumps and bumps but I don't care!

I'm not up here because of how I look but because of who I am. *Maddy Blue* – the one with the bright ideas! That feels just fine.

Next thing I know, some cheesy conga music starts up and Scott and Starr are trying to get me to join in.

The Head's got the camera and when I reach out for it he says, 'Don't worry, I'll film it from here. You've been behind the scenes long enough, Maddy. Time to go and join your friends.'

Scott's conga-ing away in front of me so I grab hold of him and Starr hangs on from behind. We join the line of kids, parents, students and teachers dancing round the hall and out into the grounds and I don't feel like Maddy the Misfit any more, that sad mag-hag who thought her only friends were magazines...

I suppose I've learned that there's more to life than glossy girl-world but that doesn't mean I won't carry on reading mags. They're fun if you don't take them too seriously and sometimes you catch something that spookily seems to be written especially for you.

Like now, just when I've quit being a jealousy junkie it looks like Starr might have to move on again. And I'll miss her so much, even though I've still got Scott.

So, it's a good thing I checked out Lifecoach Laura this week. She's doing a feature about how to survive when friends move away which looks like the perfect thing for me.

There's even a *Top Tips for Long Distance Friendships,* which I'm going to cut out and keep.

I only hope I won't need it…

GOTHIC GODDESS

WHAT'S IN THE NEXT ISSUE OF MADDY?

Maddy Blue walks on the Dark Side!
Another True Confessions special

Starr visits London! – Exclusive Fashion shoot

Love is in the air – find our where!!!!!

Scott speaks out – lad mag pages

Turn the page to see some more Orchard Books you might enjoy...

978 1 84121 435 1

£4.99

WARNING!

Snoopers watch out!

Fierce guard-bunny on patrol!

So paws off this book!

That includes my friend, Cassie. And especially MUM. Who's FAR too busy drooling over creepy-crawly Action Man to care about what I think anyway.

Shortlisted for the Sheffield Children's Book Award

Pat Moon

Loads of secret stuff about BOYS, worry bugs, babies, enemies, etcetera, etcetera.

Snoopers will be savaged by Twinkle (warrior-princess guinea pig).

978 1 84121 810 6 £4.99

Emily Smith

Jeff really liked television. Cartoons were more interesting than life. Sit-coms were funnier than life. And in life you never got to watch someone trying to ride a bike over an open sewer. Sometimes at night Jeff even dreamed television. Mum complained, but it didn't make any difference. Jeff didn't take any notice of her, which was a mistake.

A very funny and thought-provoking book from Emily Smith, winner of two Smarties Prizes.

Utterly Me, Clarice Bean

By Lauren Child

978 1 84362 304 5

£4.99 (utterly worth it)

This is me, Clarice Bean.
Mrs Wilberton, my teacher, wants us to do a book project – which sounds utterly dreary... until I find out there is an actual prize. Me and my utterly best friend, Betty Moody, really want to win...but how?

'An utterly fantastic book.' The Sunday Times

'Very entertaining.' The Independent

'Feisty and free-wheeling. Hilarious and irresistible.' The Financial Times

Other Orchard Books you might enjoy

Clarice Bean Spells Trouble	Lauren Child	978 1 84362 858 3*
The Truth Cookie	Fiona Dunbar	978 1 84362 549 0*
Cupid Cakes	Fiona Dunbar	978 1 84362 688 6
Chocolate Wishes	Fiona Dunbar	978 1 84362 689 3*
Clair de Lune	Cassandra Golds	978 1 84362 926 9
The Truth about Josie Green	Belinda Hollyer	978 1 84362 885 9
Hothouse Flower	Rose Impey	978 1 84616 215 2
My Scary Fairy Godmother	Rose Impey	978 1 84362 683 1
Shooting Star	Rose Impey	978 1 84362 560 5
Forever Family	Gill Lobel	978 1 84616 211 4*
Seventeen Times as High as the Moon	Livi Michael	978 1 84362 726 5
Do Not Read – Or Else	Pat Moon	978 1 84616 082 0

All priced at £4.99 except those marked * which are £5.99

Orchard Red Apples are available from all good bookshops,
or can be ordered direct from the publisher:
Orchard Books, PO BOX 29, Douglas IM99 1BQ
Credit card orders please telephone 01624 836000
or fax 01624 837033
or visit our Internet site: www.wattspub.co.uk
or e-mail: bookshop@enterprise.net for details.

To order please quote title, author and ISBN
and your full name and address.
Cheques and postal orders should be made payable to 'Bookpost plc.'
Postage and packing is FREE within the UK
(overseas customers should add £1.00 per book).

Prices and availability are subject to change.